# DATING THE DUKE

## JEN GEIGLE JOHNSON

# INTRODUCTION

Sign up on her website for newsletter freebies, contests, prizes and first news. http://www.jengeiglejohnson.com.
Or to Join her ARC team, follow her FB group.

Other historical books by Jen:

The Nobleman's Daughter
Two lovers in disguise

Scarlet
The Pimpernel retold

Tabitha's Folly
Childhood friends. Four Protective Brothers

Damen's Secret
The villain's romance

Dating the Duke
Time Travel: Regency man in NYC

Anthologies
A Christmas Courting
A Yuletide Regency
To Kiss A Billionaire

Check out these fun Sweet Contemporary Romance Titles:
The Swoony Sports Romances
Hitching the Pitcher
Falling for Centerfield
Charming the Shortstop
Snatching the Catcher
Flirting with First
Kissing on Third

Her Billionaire Royals Series:
The Heir
The Crown
The Duke
The Duke's Brother
The Prince
The American
The Spy
The Princess

Her Billionaire Cowboys Series:
Her Billionaire Cowboy
Her Billionaire Protector
Her Billionaire in Hiding

Her Billionaire Christmas Secret
Her Billionaire to Remember

Her Love and Marriage Brides Series
The Bride's Secret
The Bride's Cowboy
The Bride's Billionaire

Her Single Holiday Romances
Taming Scrooge

# PROLOGUE

### The Magic

*F*ive sisters gathered in Nellie's front room. The faerie looked as normal as she ever did, though the air shimmered around her, and she smelled ancient. Not old or weathered, more like stone or the sky. The women also shimmered, but not with magic. The energy, the expectation of traveling through time rushed through them, evidenced in their smiles, the movement of their feet, their clutching hands, their giggles. At last their youngest, Julia, had experienced the magic. Lady Anna squeezed her sister's hand. "Just wait until you try modern ice cream."

The others shivered in excitement. "New York City, here we come!" Constance ran her hands up and down her arms.

Bethany's lower lip appeared. "I so wanted her to see 1793."

"Oh stop, Bethany. She'll meet your Henri soon enough." Lady Anna waved her hand. They all turned to the fae.

Nellie eyed the women to her front. Of all the mortals she helped on their way, these were powerful: sisters, united, determined. She smiled, knowing what lay ahead. She addressed the youngest. "Twickenham Manor is a magical place. I'm sure you've noticed." Nellie sat on the edge of the sofa and reached for the tea cart, rolling it closer. The young woman sitting beside her had the same frightened look, the same disbelieving shock she'd seen many times over the centuries. "Would you like some sugar in your tea? Or maybe lemon or cream?"

Julia looked at Nellie vacantly. "Cream, please." Her eyes wandered the room.

"Of course." Nellie prepared the cup and passed it to her. "And a scone?" She held the tray out, but Julia shook her head.

Nellie poured herself a cup and tipped it to her lips.

Julia did the same. At the first sip, her eyes widened, and then she gulped the rest down. Her shoulders relaxed, lowered. "Better."

Nellie's special blend of tea, and the spark of magic she brewed it with, helped with everyone's acceptance.

"Have I truly gone to another time?" Julia shook her head.

"Time isn't linear at all. Every person has their own thread. When your thread touches another time, well, there you are. Or rather, here you are."

"I can't stay here. I have to go back." She set her cup on the tray, turning to her sisters. "How can you just leave? There is the estate. The tenants."

Before they could answer, Nellie clucked. "On the next full moon, you can return to the exact moment you left. You'll miss nothing. Or you can stay here. Or you can go to another time." Nellie stood with her and walked her and her family to the door. "The magic has chosen you. You have one month to decide." The sisters shivered again and gathered around the youngest.

One of Nellie's fae servants met them, and Nellie sent the new traveler off with the promise of adventure and love, then walked back to her seat, waiting for the next to arrive as they always did, in every century.

She was always there, guardian of the magic.

# CHAPTER 1

*J*ane Sullivan stretched her arms up over her head, the words "Find your Darcy" tweaked in a wonky distorted fold across her chest. She pulled her T-shirt tight again, tucking the ends into her jeans.

Abby, the girl at her neighboring cubicle, peeked over the top. "Hurry! Bring up the next one." She checked to make sure their supervisor wasn't watching and then motioned for Jane to move faster.

Jane laughed and clicked on the Twickenham Regency Reenactment House Party.

*Male Guests.*

Across her computer screen scrolled one man in Regency breeches after another, this year's guests. Ever since she'd read *Austenland* by Shannon Hale, she'd been dreaming of this particular vacation. Two weeks pretending to live in Regency England, a reenactment even her active imagination couldn't dream up better than it already sounded. Her Jane Austen heart danced a quadrille at the thought.

Jane was named after Miss Austen and was well versed

in all her books, her journals, her life story, her home; Jane Austen's very thoughts, were they available, would have been memorized. Jane Sullivan loved her Jane Austen. She owned a pair of Colin Firth earrings, frequently asked herself, "What would Jane say?" and was determined—forced herself—to like tea. She just couldn't do the watered-down variety. Every cup had to have three tea bags or it had no kick. She didn't know how anyone could handle it any other way. Surely no one liked hot water with a mild taste of dirt. Tea must taste like something.

She reached for her certificate on the wall of her cubicle, the one listing her master's in British history. Jane Sullivan was now a touted expert on Jane Austen. People sought her opinion about all things Jane, and she happily obliged them. In fact, she was well into her doctorate work and had outlined a thesis, of course, Jane Austen related.

She clicked on the next set of men who would be in attendance.

The ladies from the office crowded around her cubicle. "Ooh . . . Mmm . . . Hmm. He's your guy."

"No, did you see that last one? The redhead has my vote."

"Are these the men who will be there for sure or just hired models to advertise the place?" The entire office of twelve simmered with jealousy. They would. Because they all worked at the Jane Austen Center for Historical Studies, New York office. But no one was as dedicated to the subject as Jane Sullivan.

"Yes, that's what the site says, and the women too. Everyone you see here is an attendee this year." Jane clicked on the next man, and even she felt her breathing pick up. She had been saving for a year and had purchased the tickets months ago.

Then the center had offered to sponsor some of the trip if she used the time for research.

They would all live on an estate in England and participate in an authentic house party, just like they used to hold in the nineteenth century. The location boasted a team of regular actors. They were the staff, the butler, the servants, and occasionally a participant to even out numbers. But the vacation asked for singles only and was an effective matchmaking event. Each guest posted their picture in historical clothing online, and they all communicated with each other with fake names and titles ahead of time. What kind of man would agree to such a vacation? Willingly go? She wanted that kind of man.

She clicked on the newest attendee to post a picture of himself in Regency attire.

The ladies shouted, "What! Tell me you're not gonna be all over that one."

Jane shook her head. "It's the breeches. Look. Imagine him in gym shorts. Not the same effect." But as she scrutinized his broad shoulders and scruffy chin, she knew he'd be hot in any clothing. She was counting down the hours until her flight left for England in the morning.

Her boss peeked around the corner of the cubicle. "Jane, can I have a word?" Her amused glance at everyone told them she would forgive the break from work, but they knew they had better return to their own desks.

Jane followed Chelsea to her office. They'd been friends for ten years, went to undergrad together, and both majored in the same program, history.

Once Chelsea shut the door, she turned and squealed. "I'm so excited for you. You have to tell me everything."

"I wish you were coming."

"We can't very well send two of us on this trip." She sat

down and motioned for Jane to do the same. "Take all sorts of pictures. And remember your research."

Jane nodded. "Believe it or not, I am most excited about the research." This particular house neighbored one that preserved a rare set of old documents, journals, and artwork that could lend support to the group's research and also to Jane's dissertation. Chatwick Manor was the home of a family of daughters for many years. And it was their journals Jane was after. And, for personal reasons, one particular painting.

"Is Trent okay with all this?" Chelsea's eyes held concern, and Jane knew she wanted the two of them to get back together, but Jane had given up on Trent a month ago. "We broke up. You know that. He doesn't get to have an opinion."

Chelsea sighed. "I know. I thought for sure you guys would make it."

"You just like him with his shirt off." She laughed. "He's getting way too big." At first as a hobby, Trent had started entering bodybuilding contests and weight lifting exhibitions. He took up modeling and continued to work on his physique until Jane looked at him and all she saw were huge defined muscles, even in places she didn't know had actual muscle tissue. The hobby became an obsession and took over his life like it did his body.

"Then you're free! Get over Trent in the arms of a hottie in Regency costume."

Jane grinned. "You know I will!" Was it normal to wish you lived in a different age? Jane did, or rather, she wished men and women behaved together now more like they did back then. She could certainly do without the chamber pots and leeches, but she loved the genteel way they behaved and the lovely manner in which they treated each other.

After work, Jane hurried home so that she could finish

packing. When she walked in the door to her apartment, the cat rubbed her ankles and the fish aquarium bubbled, but everything was too quiet. As always, she wished for her fictional lady's maid to appear and pack her trunk. Procrastinating, she pulled a book off her shelf. Her guilty pleasure. Some women did online dating, read romance novels, or hung out in bars, but Jane, she kept going back to one picture in an old historical book on artwork in the Regency time period. Was she insane? Who knew, but she wanted to look at him again, her authentic Regency man.

Page 42. The book fell open to the spot. 1817. A painting of two people in a crowded room where others were dancing. They were dressed in Regency attire. But the woman was not looking at her partner. Her neck was craned to check out another man standing in the corner with a smug look on his face. He knows something. The woman clutches a piece of paper to her breast. No historian had been able to determine the message in the painting, nor the identity of the man in the corner.

The woman craning her neck was likely one of the sisters in the house near where Jane would be staying in a few days. Jane ran a hand down the page, stopping on the man in the corner. "Who are you?" Something about his face. She was drawn to him, pulled into their story, and she hoped she could find out just what he was thinking. Of course he was also handsome. She was first drawn to his sharp jawline, his thick dark hair, his broad shoulders. He looked like the football player of Regency men. But the longer she stared at his image, the more she wanted to know what went on behind those blue eyes. What would they look like if staring into her own?

He was akin to the *Mona Lisa* of the Regency historical world. His smug smile, his secretive glance, the note in the woman's hand. Jane wasn't the only person fascinated with the mystery. *What makes this man smile?* Her finger lingered on his face. *Was she nuts to find him attractive?* How often had she imagined that instead of leaning against the wall, he was dancing with her, the waltz, around and around in that dance hall? She put the book in her trunk.

Her phone dinged. A Facebook message from the new guy coming to Twickenham.

What? Her fingers shook as she slid open the notification.

*I think, of everyone, you and I are uniquely participating for research purposes. Look forward to exchanging ideas.*

Mmm. Now that was the perfect opening. She typed back. *I as well. I arrive tomorrow. Lunch the following?*

Meet outside the event? She wasn't sure of the rules, but she suspected they were supposed to meet for the first time in character and in costume.

Three dots indicated he was typing a response. After many minutes, he said, *Going rogue?*

She laughed. *No, just intrigued by your research.*

*Ah, a fellow curious mind.*

They made all the arrangements for meeting and set up lunch for when she arrived. She couldn't resist and added, *Breeches welcome but not required.* She hit send and then cringed. That could be taken many ways . . . How could she be making breeches comments to a stranger? She was hanging out with her office mates too often.

But he immediately sent a laughing emoji and said, *Breeches for enactment ONLY.*

She breathed out in relief. *Pity . . . see you in a couple days.*

So many things to look forward to, and a new lunch date on top of it all. Life couldn't be any more exciting if she had written herself in her own novel.

# CHAPTER 2

*A*lgernon Ramsbury shouted to his friends across the park in a most uncouth manner. He'd been called uncouth more often than his own title for most of his life, and while its use may have bothered him when he was young, he now felt little regard for any who chose to use such a word. Those two syllables spoke far more about the person speaking than the one being described.

For one, people speaking the word *uncouth* had pinched lips. What was to be enjoyed about pinched lips? Pinched lips rarely smiled. They had a tightness about them, and several rows of vertical wrinkles lining the mouth. He grimaced. But the worst part about pinched lips was the impossibility of kissing them properly. Whoever heard of enjoying the hard ball of pinched lips under their own? He shuddered and then, to help him forget the horrific image, laughed as loud as he could.

"Tallyho!" He urged his horses faster around the next corner, thrilling in the jump his stomach made with the acceleration. Jameson tailed behind, but he was known to pull a fast trick or two at the very end and win. *Not this time.* Algernon would come out first or else be forced to dance with Winifred Wallflower at Almack's on Thursday. And he would not dance with Winifred. He urged his horses faster.

She was not so horribly repulsive. She, by herself, was actually quite plain, nothing remarkable about her. But as soon as one of the men danced with her, the talk, the expectation, the mothers hovering about would be unbearable, and none of his set wished such a thing upon themselves. If she were a new debutante, the action would not be discussed more than once or twice during a ball, but now that she had three years on the shelf, any attention at all was analyzed from all aspects and debated upon. And the matrons were already all in a ruffle about whom his ducal self might marry. He hummed. No, he must not lose this race.

But the park was beginning to attract visitors. He and his friends had meant to already be finished with their raucous behavior—his mother called it uncouth *and* raucous. By this hour they should have been safely ensconced at White's or promenading with the ladies on paths. But Roderick had arrived late, as was his habit, and none of them wished to give up on the race entirely, and so they shortened it a bit with hopes they could avoid foot traffic. Alas, people in the park were difficult to avoid at this hour. He swerved precariously away from one as a punctuation of his thoughts.

He hurried toward the next bend, way too close to a group of ladies. Several squealed, with hands over their mouths and wide, fearful eyes. Some feather of sense crept into his brain and he grappled with it for a half breath, and then he slowed. *No.* He would have to be the one to take the dripper and dance with Winifred. Someone was bound to get hurt at this pace.

Horses pounded the earth behind him, Roderick calling out, "Whoa, now. Easy, girls."

Algernon turned to him and Jameson with a shrug of his shoulders. "What's a gentleman to do?" He ignored Roderick's victorious smile and then urged his horses to a walk across the clearing to the group of ladies on his left. He bowed as gallantly as he could from a curricle while sitting down. "Good morning."

They tittered about; they giggled; a few curtsied; but none responded. His gaze traveled over the bunch of them, and dash it all, he hadn't been introduced to a single one. Well, no matter. They seemed a silly enough group; he could be grateful he avoided them one and all. Could he find but one woman brave enough to speak her mind in all of England?

Surely they did not all occupy themselves morning till night with such vacuous thoughts as needlepoint and the weather? It seemed to him that's all they ever discussed.

He'd been spoiled with friends growing up, ladies who said all manner of fascinating things, took him on frequent fantastical imaginary adventures, and stood up to his nonsense.

He clucked his tongue and guided his two horses home. What he would love to find is a woman who could challenge him, a woman with whom he could discuss things, someone who could help manage his estates, a confidante. And soft lips. He smirked. But so far, none of the vapid, eyelash-fluttering, "accomplished" women seemed to have any amount of education or practice in discussing important things. They were experts in all the dealings of others, knew just how to discuss the weather for hours on end, and could smile charmingly in support of whatever he said, be it of interest to them personally or not. Maybe he should blame the governesses. As soon as women took to the dance floor or sat in morning rooms for callers, they seemed to lose all semblance of personality. He sighed. The stable boy took his conveyance at the front door, and Algernon stepped inside.

Wailing met his ears immediately. "Go get His Grace! Fetch him for me, Doris!"

His mother's much encumbered and fettered maid rushed into the hall and nearly barreled into his chest. At times he regretted his massive height and broad chest, for they scared most servants and a good portion of the young ladies. If not his title of duke, his size surely forced them into a silent shell or to silly giggling nonsense. Neither of which he could abide.

"What is it, Doris?"

"It's your mother."

"I hear that. What precisely is the ailment?" With his mother, it was always best not to become too caught up in her complaints, for her wailing could be for a cause as terrible as she pronounced or one not nearly so awful, depending on her state of the day. Which he couldn't begin to guess, for he'd left long before she typically arose.

Doris couldn't answer the simplest of questions, and he didn't blame her. Perhaps she should get another increase in her wages. Dealing with his mother all day and into the night seemed an unfortunate existence for any human.

He hated to think of her so, but his mother was so very tiresome. Nothing was ever simple. They must make the largest to-do about every such thing that they talked about, every subject addressed, and she was the worst of gossips. He bored instantly when she was cheerfully and spitefully picking apart the faults of all the people they knew.

When Doris proved useless as a manner in which to gain information, he mercifully dismissed her. "Thank you, Doris. That will be all."

Her eyes widened in hope.

"Yes, why don't you check on Cook in the kitchen for a moment or two?" He raised his eyebrows with a slight smile on his lips.

"Thank you, Your Grace." Her curtsy was so plumb full of happiness she could have toppled over in front of him. Then she turned and hurried as fast as her stocky form allowed. He chuckled, amused.

A footman across the hall snorted.

Algernon's gaze shot up in pleased surprise. Who had dared to laugh?

Three footmen, standing at attention, were stiff and still and all held the same masque of indifference. He eyed them with suspicion. One of them might actually have a personality. He now vowed to discover who it could be.

"Doooris!" The caterwauling of his mother behind the parlor doors beckoned. "Doris, oh Doris!"

He adjusted his jacket, held his chin high, and then nodded that the door should be opened.

"Dorisss—Oh, son. *Son*, I am so happy to see you."

"Hello, Mother. How are you this fine morning?" He smiled as widely as he could, hoping his joviality would rub off.

"Not well. Not well at all. I have the suffering, the exquisite torture, of one who will never see her loved one again."

"Are you discussing Father?" He knew she was not, but he couldn't help but needle her if only a small amount.

"What! No, I didn't miss him one moment while he was on this earth. Why should I care he has since passed?"

He cringed and regretted his callous tormenting. "So tell me, Mother, who are you suffering over this morning?"

She sucked in a long shaky breath and let it out slowly. "Our. Dear. Mugsy."

Praise be! Could the dog have finally gone the way of all miserable pugs? "What has happened to our much celebrated Mugsy?"

"Missing. No one knows where he is, and I long for his company."

He lifted his eyes to a footman. "Has anyone called for a runner?"

"No, Your Grace."

"The magistrate? Is he aware?"

"No, Your Grace."

"Then perhaps you can tell me just what has been done in our search for Mugsy?" He kept a straight face, with only the slight wiggle of his lips in betrayal of his desire to laugh.

The footman bowed. "A search is underway as we speak, Your Grace. He has not been located in any of Her Grace's rooms, the hallways, or the kitchen."

Algernon nodded. "And the search is still underway, I assume?"

"Yes, Your Grace."

"And you will not desist until you have found the pug?"

"We will not."

He nodded to his mother. "There, you see. He shall be found! For our staff would not countenance the idea of disappointing you." Could he have imagined it, or did the footman wince? What had become of his staff, wincing in his presence, losing all semblance of decorum? "And now, we shall dab our eyes, clear our throats. Ahem." He handed his mother one of his handkerchiefs. "Wipe our noses and carry on with heads held high, for we have a dinner party, do we not?"

"Oh we do! Oh good heavens. Oh my glory. We have a dinner party." She fanned herself, and Algernon left the room firm in the knowledge that she would actively torment other members of the household clear until the dinner hour.

When he exited his mother's parlor room, the doors shut behind him and he took but two steps before he stalled in his movement and simply had nothing else to do. He turned to the nearest footman. "What does a new duke, younger than any duke ought to be, do with his extra time, dear footman?"

The man bowed in the small space between them, which Algernon found admirable. Quite a feat, actually, if he pondered the stiff stance required for such an expression of respect. "Might I suggest White's?"

He was no use. Algernon nodded. "I see. Not much different from when I was merely the son of a duke. So, when home becomes unbearably dull, dukes horde together with drinks and games to amuse them?"

The footman did not respond, probably assuming the question rhetorical, and Algernon suspected it was. But he desperately needed a distraction from all his looming responsibilities. The estate books awaited him. Already many months a duke, and Algernon still could not face his father's dreaded books. The steward, the solicitor, his father's secretary all wished to speak to him, but he had been sloughing them off for nigh on four months now. Perhaps he should venture in to look at the study, peek at a few pages to see what was required.

Before forcing movement from his feet, he spoke again to the footman. "It seems Mugsy is hiding from his mistress. Will you send someone to the east garden? He suns himself against the wall there."

The nearest footman bowed again and went to carry out Algernon's request.

*Now, the study.* He turned in that direction. After four steps, dread made his feet so heavy he would have halted the journey altogether if the staff weren't witnessing. He forced one foot in front of the other, turned the corner, and almost ran away, down the hall and out of sight. But instead he took a step into his father's domain.

The room smelled of the man. Which Algernon found interesting. He did not have any reaction at all to the smell, good or bad, just a recognition of it. He had the absurd notion that perhaps his father would recognize his son's smell in the same manner were the duke to ever venture in Algernon's old study on the opposite side of the house. Were he to in fact recognize even his bedchambers, were he to know Algernon's course of study at Oxford, or were he to even be able to guess at Algernon's horse's name. He supposed one could not grieve too much a father one did not see or interact with. He ventured over to the chair. It sat opposite the desk, on the side not meant for Algernon, the side where old men, old dukes, sat and knew how to do things.

But he walked around the desk, trailing his fingers as he went, running them along the rough grain of the wood, and before he could stop himself out of fear, sat in the very seat his father had occupied almost every time he saw the man. If he weren't such an intelligent child, he might have wondered in his younger years if the chair were in fact attached to his father's person or if his father slept there, for he never once remembered the man in any other location.

Which he knew to be ridiculous. Surely his father entertained guests, spoke to others at dinner parties, attended balls, but Algernon would have been in the nursery during those moments. His memories were sadly limited. And then his parents had shipped him off to school, Eton, then he finished Oxford, and then home for the funeral. And his new title. And months on end of tedium, frozen in fear of a responsibility that felt larger than even England itself.

As his backside settled into the chair, he laughed. This was not so bad. He could venture to sit here now and again as long as he didn't have to do anything. Then a knock. "Enter." His voice squeaked. He thought squeaking voices ended during his formative years at Eton. He cleared his throat. "Enter," he called in his deepest bass.

The door cracked. "A Mr. Pendleton to see you, Your Grace."

His mouth went dry. Wasn't Mr. Pendleton the solicitor? He raised his brows in question, and the butler nodded. And clarified. "The solicitor."

Algernon swallowed. "And how is it that the moment, the very second I sit in this chair, he is at my door?"

"I don't know, Your Grace. Might I say, I find it curious myself?"

Algernon nodded again. "And I don't suppose I could refuse him?"

"You could, but it would not be advised, Your Grace. Begging your pardon, Your Grace, and if I'm out of line, I do apologize, but I believe your father mentioned some urgent matters to be discussed with the solicitor?"

He sat back. What harm could it do, to talk to the man? He would need to discuss whatever it was sometime, and with his steward as well. Hopefully the steward could handle most things until Algernon felt like doing something for the estate.

A tall man with a long nose entered the room, all smiles and greeting.

Algernon would have doubted his reliability in the face of being too cheery had Mr. Pendleton not been much celebrated as a competent fellow.

As soon as Mr. Pendleton sat, he said, "Your Grace, I am so pleased you would receive me, for I have news."

Algernon leaned forward. "News?" He was cursed with a curiosity that burned an eternal flame and was never quenched. He found so little of intrigue in London that just the mention of news from Mr. Pendleton set his brain on fire. "Is it the good sort?"

"The very best, the life-changing sort." His eyes sparkled with an energy Algernon found even more curious.

"Then do tell, Mr. Pendleton. I regret not seeing you sooner."

"I may only give you a portion of the news here, for I don't have details. The rest will come when you attend *this* house party." He slid a parchment sealed with purple wax across the table to Algernon.

Curious. He had never seen such a seal, people with wings? Purple wax? It seemed a shame to break it, but he did. He scanned the page. All looked unremarkable. He was invited to a house party. To Twickenham Manor, an estate near that of his dear childhood friends. He was to respond with his acceptance as soon as possible. He lifted his gaze again to the mysterious Mr. Pendleton. "And I will receive the rest of this most curious good news when I arrive?"

"That you will, and if my sources are to be believed, it is the best kind of news indeed."

# CHAPTER 3

*H*er flight landed in Heathrow. She tapped her feet in excitement. The dreary clouds out the window welcomed her in a blanket of thick air. The drizzle misting her plexiglass seemed a shower of sunshine to her England-hungry heart. She craned her neck to see the front of the airplane. The only thing between her and the bliss of Britain's green shores was a plane full of people slowly standing and stretching and waiting to unload in front of her. Nothing created more loathing in Jane's heart for her fellow humans than a plane full of people unloading. Could it not be done in a quicker manner? Why the standing for a full ten minutes before the door even opened? The envy for a first class seat was always strongest at this moment, when waiting to exit. She'd never sat in the front, never thought she would, but always, in moments of unloading, she dreamed of that first seat. 1A. Maybe one day she would sit in 1A and leave the plane as soon as the door opened.

She smiled inside. *Maybe.* If she could finish this doctorate with something truly original, if what she suspected these letters held panned out as she hoped, then she was going to fly somewhere in seat 1A.

Her research. She knew there were women in the Regency and Georgian eras who were strong leaders, innovative, even. But they performed their acts of societal rebellion within the constraints of the time. She would prove it. Her inner tribute to Jane Austen and her characters made her smile. Jane would further what she thought Miss Austen's work began, showing the true power and strength of women. If not, she would be out of a job and her whole historical society shut down. No pressure or anything.

As it was, today, she sat in 34C. She twisted to stand, but she was too tall and ducked under the overhead compartment. No room in the aisle for another person. The air vent pressure streamed cold air into the top of her head. She sighed and sat back down.

The speaker turned on with the captain's faraway and almost unintelligible voice. There was some difficulty with the landing bridge, and he asked everyone to retake their seats and wait patiently until it was resolved. Her outer pleasant reserve belied her inner impatience at the delay. But a text chimed. Dr. Smithy, her lunch date. *Welcome to England. I assume you have landed and are enjoying the dreary weather?*

Already feeling better, she smiled. *Landed. Looks perfectly lovely from my airplane window. Unfortunately still on the plane. As of yet, still planning on lunch.*

*Oh, the pitfalls of commercial travel.*

Interesting. Did he often find himself on private jets? *Shall I let you know if we delay further?*

*An enticing woman full of interesting conversation is worth waiting for. Just let me know.*

Oh, he said all the right things. She screenshotted his last comment and whipped it off to Chelsea, who responded immediately with a row full of hearts. Then the captain announced the door was open and they would soon be exiting the craft. At last.

She rented a car, wanting to embrace left side of the road driving and because she really wanted to be free to explore, but her palms were sweating and her mouth dry by the time she finally reached the hotel. Maybe she would leave the car in parking and pay for a driver for the rest of her time. Three weeks in glorious England. Two at the Twickenham retreat and one to do with as she wished.

Her hotel room was quaint. They made a real effort at authentic historical England, she would give them that. She would stay in it one night before she checked in at Twickenham tomorrow. Her body hummed with excitement, then stress. What should she wear to her lunch? Business? Should she scream research expert? Or sexy lady of intelligence? Was that even a thing? *Sexy lady of intelligence.* She laughed at her own ridiculous train of thought. Probably to Dr. Smithy. Academics always thought smart women were sexy . . . the younger academics. The older crowd needed a refresher course on precisely what a woman was doing as faculty in their university or running research think tanks. Dr. Smithy would arrive in twenty minutes. At last, she decided to go with a mix between the two: sexy, smart, flirty fun. She slipped into a pink dress and strappy sandals and freshened her makeup. Powder, a little lipstick, and mascara did wonders for a woman. Oh, what she could do for all those women during the Regency time period. She'd always wished to do a couple of makeovers. Subtle. Men would be falling at their feet. She giggled.

So few knew the extent of her nerdiness. Even the gals at work paled in comparison to the amount of passion and attention she dedicated to one relatively small year span of the Regency period in the Georgian era in England. She had to nail the research on this trip. They were all counting on her.

Satisfied she would impress a studious man interested in educated conversation, as well as a self-assured man who looked much better than anyone had a right to in Regency-era breeches, she made her way downstairs to the lobby.

She searched the crowd, trying to remember him from the picture he posted.

Then Darcy himself entered through the front door and she forgot everything else. He wasn't wearing breeches, but his hair, his bearing, his suitcoat. *Mmm.* Chiseled jaw, superb cut on his jacket, broad shoulders, deep eyes—eyes that were watching her, amused, while she checked him out.

She felt her face heat, but instead of looking away like a shy teenager, she smiled and made her way over to him. As soon as she approached, he held out his hand, "Jane Sullivan?"

Caught by surprise, she stammered before her brain connected. "You must be Dr. Smithy?"

"The very same. But please, call me Charles."

*Oh, his voice.* She might pass out from the shivers that raced up her back from such a deep voice speaking the lovely accent of the upper classes. Maybe she could convince him to read her stories, Jane Austen stories. He would be the voice of Darcy from now on in her head when she read. Her face heated even further when she realized the implications of her thoughts.

He waited, eyebrow still raised, and she stammered again. Then cleared her throat. "Thank you. For meeting me. Going rogue, as you said." She laughed.

"My pleasure. I've followed your work. I'm delighted to spend the time, and besides I think once the retreat begins we will be in character and perhaps not at liberty to have such lengthy research-related conversations?"

She nodded. "True. I'm looking forward to it. I've always thought this kind of hands-on research into the culture and time of the Regency era most productive."

"And I as well, and the neighborhood where we are staying holds some interesting treasures, I presume." His eyes watched her. A glint of something more than idle conversation made her want to impress him, show him all that she knew.

But he held out his arm, "Shall we?"

She placed a hand on his forearm. *So Regency.* Her grin probably cracked her face as he led her through the lobby.

He chuckled, "You are a true follower."

"Of all things Jane? You know it."

"I often wish people would treat each other with the same manners, the same gentility as the bon ton is reported to have done."

He said all the right things.

He led her out the front door of the hotel and to a waiting limousine. "I find it much more pleasant to let someone else do the driving."

"Oh, I can't tell you how much I agree. I tried to do it myself, rented a car, wanted to acclimate, have the freedom of my own wheels kind of thing. Ugh. I'm afraid I'm an expected embarrassment to my nation." She indicated the waiting car. "This is more my plan moving forward." Though she was not thinking limousine, more like whatever the British used as taxis.

"You are welcome to make use of my driver for any side trips you need while you're here."

Dare she? What a temptation! What a boon. "What? Oh thank you. That is more than generous, and I may take him up on your offer more than he is willing to humor me. I think you'll find I have an insatiable curiosity. Especially for England."

"I too share your appetite . . ." His eyes lit with suggestion, and her face warmed. "For knowledge."

She laughed.

They made themselves comfortable on the same seat facing forward. "I'm sincere in my offer. You can't wear him out. He'll be happy to oblige." He offered her a water bottle. "But I do hope for some of your excursions, you will be accepting of my company?"

"Oh, of course. I wouldn't want to intrude on your plans, but I'd enjoy your company. Very much." *Ugh. Did the word "very" just come out of my mouth?* If she were home, she would have slapped her own forehead. She'd have to up her game of witty conversation if she was going to hold her own at this party.

They arrived at a cottage-looking restaurant. The cobble-stone walk, the stone on the walls, the original wood sign that hung at the front door. Charles was smooth, charming, pleasant, the perfect gentleman. Every time her water lowered, he motioned for it to be filled. When she rubbed her arms because of the chilly air conditioning that kicked on, he asked the server to turn it down. Everything was to her liking, or he worked to make it so.

Then, as they sat back in their seats, relaxing after a full meal, he said, "They're running a contest this year." His eyes sparkled with the energy of a secret.

"They are?" She hadn't heard. Why did he know about a contest and she didn't? A spark of competitive irritation lit. She tried to squelch the ridiculous thought and forced herself to listen.

"Yes, the person who is most authentic, best played out in experience and conversation, gets to explore a private art gallery in the neighboring Chatwick Manor and have the first peek at some older artifacts that were discovered in the attic."

Her heart beat with hope. "The Lichfield Sister letters?"

He nodded and then twirled his glass. "And I figure you and I can win this thing hands down."

The obvious problem being, they would be in competition with each other. And one thing she knew, if it was him against her, she was betting on her.

His eyebrow raised as if guessing the direction of her thoughts. "If we work together."

She lifted her chin. *Ah.* Then she smiled. "You're on."

*Until it's time to choose just one winner, and then all bets are off, no matter how much you look like Darcy.*

# CHAPTER 4

*A*lgernon stuck his head out the carriage window. "Dash it all!" Rain poured in sheets from the sky, not so much the hammering or pounding-on-the-roof kind of rain, but the silent dousing kind. His hair fell forward into his face, and rivulets ran down his collar and wet his underclothes.

His valet handed him a handkerchief to dry his face. He lifted the tiny bit of fabric, doubting its usefulness against the drenching, but he made an attempt with it anyway.

A tall manor loomed above him in the darkness. Twickenham. Intriguing. Looked like a nice enough house, large, somewhat quaint. What was this news they were to tell him? He had to admit he loved a secret. The other thing he loved about this house party was that it took him far away from his father's study and the steward. He snorted at himself. Afraid of his own steward. He sat back on his carriage bench. He imagined many a gentleman was afraid of his steward. Regular taskmasters they were. A steward meant work, and work was not altogether detestable, but the type of work one did not know how to crawl out of, the type of work that involved rescuing one's estate from ruin, that kind of work was unbearably oppressive and best be delayed as long as possible. Which Algernon planned to do.

When they pulled to the front, a footman opened his door and waited with an umbrella. Rain still poured from the sky in one continuous sheet. He sucked in his breath, gritted his teeth, and then stepped out into it. They hurried to the front steps and he rushed inside, ready for a crackling fire, warm tea with spirits, and a nice bed.

The entry was dark. And cold. No one stood ready to greet him. One candle flickered on an entryway table. He wasn't very late in arriving. Perhaps nine in the evening. The footman brought his trunk into the entryway and waited. Algernon was aghast that no one had come forward to greet him. No one stood at the door. He was of a mind to call out into the house, but at length a pale and waif-like maid curtsied before him and handed him a note. Then she scampered away as if avoiding harm. "What the blazes?" He tore open the paper, his infrequent temper rising a notch as he skimmed a hastily written missive. "Your room is at the top of the stairs, fourth door down." He turned the paper over in his hand. No other message to be found. Grumbling, he made his way toward the stairs. "Follow me." His valet and footman stepped behind him.

The same maid returned with a candle in her hand.

He followed her up the stairs but had to pause, bouncing with one foot on a step. "Your stairs don't creak."

"Pardon me, Your Grace?"

"They don't creak. They look older than any staircase ought to look, but see." He bounced. "No noise." He continued up the steps. "These seem brand new to walk upon."

She turned, but not before he saw the hint of a small, secretive sort of smile on her lips.

"You know something."

She didn't respond.

"It's all part of this secret, isn't it?" He followed her. "The news?"

She remained silent but led him down the hallway at the top of the stairs. When she stopped at his door, he mumbled, "Thank you." And she disappeared as quietly as she had come.

His valet set about unpacking while Algernon waited for some sustenance. He was quite fatigued, and his stomach rumbled and ached with hunger.

He moved to the fireplace to take the edge off of his cold. He immediately warmed. What a lovely fire. He peered closer to see, or even smell, the type of wood. Perhaps to warm up his own fires at home. He shook his head and peeked down, almost singing his eyebrows from the heat. The fireplace, though burning brightly in flames, showed no signs of black ash or of a history of use. Curious. Their nonexistent staff worked miracles on the fireplace, but didn't know how to welcome a guest into their home. He sniffed, growing hungrier. The place felt different, foreign to him.

He turned to do a perusal of the rest of his room. It seemed adequate. Nondescript décor. The coverlet, though in a style of long ago, seemed not to be worn at all, as though it were stitched yesterday.

The mattress felt deep and soft and yet it was firm enough that he found no trouble anticipating a pleasant night's rest. He'd begin such a welcome activity immediately were he not increasing in hunger and a comparable irritability.

"Where is our repast, Oliver?"

His valet peered around the corner from the closet. "I'm sure I don't know, Your Grace. I've had no communication from a single servant, know nothing of your schedule and, might I add, the lack of candles is deplorable."

It was so unlike the valet to complain, Algernon found his cantankerous attitude almost amusing, except that he himself was just as irritable. "I find this completely unacceptable. I will go in search of the evening meal myself." He huffed. He could use a good walk, and the place made him curious, if also a little bit wary.

As soon as he was refreshed and deemed presentable by his ever loyal valet, he made his way out into the hallway in search of his first meal.

He had walked back to the front entryway of the house by the time a servant caught sight of him. They were deplorably understaffed. Perhaps, or all early sleepers. That seemed absurd. What servant fell asleep while guests were arriving?

A young maid curtsied, "Your Grace, beg pardon. But the lady is expecting you in the library."

At last, some semblance of the expected niceties. His stomach grumbled, but he reluctantly followed the directions the servant gave him to locate the library and soon found himself at the door, which was cracked ajar. Perhaps he should knock, but a figure moving around in what he thought was an odd manner piqued his interest, and he pushed the door with his toe to broaden the crack.

A woman with white hair moved about the room in an intricate dance. It appeared to be the quadrille, perhaps, but he couldn't be sure because she danced alone, embellished the moves, and waved her arms about in such a manner that he found it difficult to exactly determine which dance she might be attempting. And there was no music in the room.

He pushed the door farther, determined to make his presence known. When a voice across the room said, "You must tell him straight away. All the signs point to him. He is the one for this travel."

"Of course I will. He has come so far already. I will let him settle first and then break the news to him gently in the morning."

Algernon cleared his throat. "What news?"

"Perhaps now would be best. You could attempt our new method even if the painting is not yet complete." The voice seemed to come from behind the back bookcase.

For the first time Algernon considered that perhaps his idea of good news and that of the solicitor might not align. His gaze traveled over the library, impressively stocked with many shelves of books, looking for the speaker from a moment ago. "Where is he?"

The woman dancer had stopped, though unashamed of her odd behavior. "Your Grace?" Her eyebrows rose, and Algernon knew he was meant to be intimidated by such an imposing, though beautiful, brow. He squinted as he stared at her. She, too, seemed timeless. He couldn't quite put an age on her. One moment he thought he saw a few wrinkles about her eyes, the next her skin was smooth. Her hair was white, or blonde, or gray.

He cleared his throat. "I was told you sought my company?"

The door behind him opened wider, and footmen brought in trays of food.

The woman indicated that he sit at a table in the corner. "Yes, thank you. As none of the other guests have arrived, I hoped we could take our repast in here?" She raised her voice at the end of the phrase as though asking a question, but she moved forward as if no response were required.

He joined her. "Thank you, I'd be delighted to join you for a meal."

After a moment or two of servants filling plates, his hostess pouring tea, and the other niceties that accompanied a lovely meal, he looked up expectantly at his eccentric companion.

She dabbed her mouth delicately. "We would like to make you an irresistible offer."

He opened his eyes as wide as they would. "I'm listening. This sounds very intriguing. Though you should know, I find few things difficult to resist. Unless they are uncomfortable to my person or cause pain or some other such unpleasant feeling."

"How would you like to go away for a while?"

His heart leaped at the thought. He would love nothing more than to go on a grand tour of the Continent. Or anywhere, to avoid his home, his responsibilities, and his title. He cleared his throat. "Might I ask where and for how long?"

"Oh come now, no need to pretend indifference. You and I both know how desperately you need the escape."

"What? How could you—"

She held up her hand. "Forgive me, Your Grace, but tonight is the night. A full moon you know."

He did not know. "A full moon, you say? Sounds rather gothic. Have you been reading Horace Wadpole's *The Castle of Otranto*, by any chance?" He had a mind to leave straightaway, pack his things, and head somewhere else. No need to return home just yet . . . But she sounded less intriguing and more dark than his tastes appreciated.

"We must come to terms now so that I can finish work in my art studio. Although we won't be needing the painting, not this time."

She made little sense. Practically *no* sense, and he was well on his way to thinking her severely addled.

"So, what will it be? Would you like to leave for a time? No one will be the wiser and no one will miss you while you're gone."

"I do think my mother might notice." He toyed with his napkin. "And Roderick, I owe him some blunt, if you know what I mean—"

She waved her hand. "Never fear. For all in your life here, it shall be as though no time has passed at all." Something about her eyes intrigued him, a knowledgeable sparkle, as if there were an absurd truth to her words. So he bit his tongue and refrained from further needling her.

Whether or not he believed the woman, he could only hope she offered some form of amusement, so he said, "And how do we accomplish such a thing? For I would dearly love to go."

She nodded, seeming satisfied. "I'll make all the arrangements. Look for a package along the west wall."

"What? Did you say on the wall?"

"Yes, or in it. I forget where it was last left, but you'll have your instructions there probably behind a stone or other such thing. By the well."

He half nodded, not sure what to think about this whole conversation. But she was still watching him expectantly. "Certainly. I will be there. Package on, or in, the wall, by the well."

If any of what she offered were true, he'd be a fool not to accept. Leave for a time? No one notice he was gone? Absolutely. But he knew it was balderdash and utter nonsense. Still, it couldn't hurt to play along. "And this secret, this reason for me attending your house party to begin with?"

She arose suddenly, and he made a move to stand as well. She waved him back down. "No, no, finish your meal. I must be off. Let the servants attend to whatever you might require. Best of luck on your journey." She turned from him, not a curtsy or a farewell, come to think of it, not an introduction either. He had no idea of even her name. Was she the hostess of the party who had sent the invitation? He could not tell. Just as her age eluded him, so did her status, even her clothing. He didn't have a clear picture in his mind of what she looked like.

He lifted his fork but found he had no more appetite. Instead he wished to make his way to the west wall immediately.

While he loved a curiosity, he found this woman's behavior a bit unsettling. At least she could have performed the niceties, an introduction, commented on the weather.

Once returned to his room, he asked for his outdoor boots, a more rugged pair of breeches and jacket, and a hat and cane. "I'll be going on an extended walk, I dare say."

His valet said nothing, but the silence in the air brimmed with the unspoken.

"Oh come man, out with it."

The tiny lift of his lip made Algernon smile. "I find it curious, Your Grace. That is all."

"I as well. But I shall see you later this evening to prepare for bed." He paused and then under his breath he mumbled, "Or I won't."

"Pardon me, Your Grace?"

"It's nothing, man. I just don't know what this woman was trying to say to me. Was she saying I will be journeying today or merely learning more about my journey?"

"Will we be traveling?"

Algernon paused, then shook his head. "No, I don't think we shall. Nothing for you to worry about. I'll go on my walk, and it shall be as if I never left." He sounded ridiculous, even to himself, as she had when she first pronounced such a bit of nonsense.

His valet finished, and Algernon was off. The weather was brisk, the sky unseasonably clear, stars everywhere he looked in the night sky. The moon brightened his path, which was chilled by the wind. Fall would come early, it seemed.

He adjusted his hat so that it would not blow off the top of his head and placed his cane carefully on the soft earth. At first he followed stone-lined paths through hedge gardens and the remains of the roses from summer. A metal gate stood open at the west end of the garden. It creaked, a soft insistent noise, every time it shifted in the wind. Through it, a lovely space between the inner gardens and a great stone wall beckoned, begging to be explored. A thrilling sense of the shadows that lurked on the other side of that slowly moving gate made him pick up his pace. He imagined this was the wall his eccentric supper partner had referred to. The area just on the other side of the gardens sat in the shadow of the great wall that lined the estate grounds. But the area was blissfully outside the wind's biting touch.

Remarkably, the wall stood taller than he did. Multiple earthy-colored stones appeared at first mossy and old, but the farther he walked, the cleaner and newer they seemed. Perhaps it took many years to construct such a wall. He imagined it would. Gathering and collecting the stone alone would be quite a feat.

Up ahead, he made out a stone well. He was to search the wall near this very well, he remembered, so he picked up his pace, feeling a bit like a man on a treasure hunt. His grin grew as he imagined what he might find. Who had hidden it? He approached the wall, running his hands along the stone, searching for a wobbling piece that might conceal a bit of mystery behind it, questioning all the while the sanity of such a quest. He hoped his hostess was not insane, for he desperately wanted there to be an adventure, a journey, an escape.

His head tingled with excitement, his hands running up and down the stones of the wall from the muddy bottom to the very top. Then the tingles sharpened, like pinpoints of needles all over his head. He reached a hand up, crying out. A soft glowing powder showered down around him, and the unmistakable sound of giggling irritated his ears.

He looked up and took note of a disappearing head—curls all around, bright eyes of a woman—high above him over the top of the wall. The world spun, and he felt his vision caving inward. *No.* Pain blocked out all other sensation or awareness. He slid to the ground, both hands gripping the hair of his head, and pulled his knees to his chest, the warm stone on the wall a distant comfort as he drifted away.

# CHAPTER 5

*J*ane spun around in a circle, and her empire-waist morning dress flowed down, covering her slippers. She had taken extra care with her hair this morning in the hotel room, and when she arrived, the owner, Nellie, had seemed impressed. Though she didn't express as much, for she was their housekeeper and this was meant to be an 1817 house party. When the butler took her wrap, a footman carried her trunks, and a maid showed her upstairs, she almost squealed with each and every accurate detail. The weeks here would pass away as if in a dream, certainly more quickly than she would like. She stood now in her bedroom, admiring the expansive lawn out the back of the manor house. She planned to drink in every delicious Regency-clad moment.

A soft knock at her door, and Jane answered, "Come in."

The girl's round face, her pleased expression, her swift curtsy, made Jane smile. "My lady. I'm Dorothy. I'm to be your lady's maid while you're here." Her eyes found the floor.

Jane couldn't believe her luck. A lady's maid. Somehow

she'd missed that detail. She rushed to the girl. "I am so pleased to meet you. So beyond happy to have a lady's maid."

Dorothy blushed, curtsied again, and said, "Of course. When we saw you hadn't brought your own, the lady of the house was happy to provide. A lady such as yourself will need help dressing and doing your hair and things. I've trained in London, know all the latest hairstyles and pomades." She curtsied again and then widened her eyes expectantly at Jane.

She squealed on the inside. Then swallowed. What did you say to your maid? "Thank you, Dorothy. My trunk is in there, I believe." Jane pointed to the walk-in closet.

"Would you like to dress for dinner?"

"Yes, can you prepare the green gown?" She was getting the hang of it.

"I can. And they'll be bringing up others to choose from as well. We can have a look when it's time to get ready."

Jane nodded. "Thank you. That would be lovely." Oh, she could get used to this. She could really, *really* get used to this. Perhaps she could look into employment here at the house. A snort escaped before she could stop it. She had a job, part of the reason she'd come, she reminded herself. And besides, one did not snort in Regency England. At least not where anyone could hear.

"Was that a snort I just heard, my lady?" The sparkling eyes of Dr. Smithy shone at her from the doorway. He rapped on the frame. "Pardon me, my lady, I came by to inquire if you would enjoy a turn about the gardens before tea?" He held his hands out and turned in a circle in all his tight waistcoat, tan breeches glory.

Her cheeks heated. "Why yes, let me grab a shawl. The wind looks like it might have a bite to it."

He nodded and stepped back, the bedroom being a scandalous place for men and women to converse together.

She rushed to the closet, and Dorothy handed her a shawl. She winked and went back to unpacking.

Jane laughed and rushed outside on the arm of Dr. Smithy. She whispered. "I see the breeches have made an appearance at last." Then she squeezed his arm. "I don't know if we've been rightfully introduced. I'm Lady Jane Sullivan from Devonshire." Naturally. Devonshire. There was no better dream place to live. She didn't even care if all the ladies present claimed to be from Darcy's seat.

"And I am Lord Smithy, the Earl of Hamblin. Not too far from where you're from. I believe our parents knew each other?" He rose an eyebrow as if trying to remember.

"They did indeed. I've heard many a tall tale of their childhood adventures."

They exited out through the back gardens. Lovely carved hedgerows surrounded them on all sides, and the remnants of roses from summer filled the air with heavenly scents. The wind picked up, and she stepped nearer to Lord Smithy.

"Are you catching cold?" His concern seemed sincere. But now that they were acting their part, she couldn't be sure. Every Regency man would be required to look after her comfort, as a gentleman. Something she hadn't considered before now. If every man here was playing the part of a true gentleman, how would she know if he was sincere?"

She shook her head. "Thank you. I'll manage for now."

"I've heard more news of the contest."

He was certainly taking the contest bit seriously. As of yet, she'd heard nothing of it at all.

"Yes, we are watched, by even the servants, to see if we break character, to see how accurate to the time we behave. If we break Regency etiquette, we must be appropriately horrified, that kind of thing. The winners will have a complete afternoon with Chatwick Manor's impressive library of artifacts, paintings, and old journals and letters."

Her mouth could have watered with yearning. "I'd love to see those letters." *And the paintings.* She suspected her Regency man might be in the bunch since the woman with the note was rumored to have been raised at Chatwick Manor.

"All we have to do is stick together and play our part."

"I can do that." She smiled at him, knowing it would be difficult to find anyone more handsome. And he was deliciously educated, plus excited about history, about Regency history. She could not have created a more perfect man if she'd written one herself.

They came across a gardener who suggested a cart with a horse might be an enjoyable manner in which to experience more of the gardens that day. "There's a bit of mud about, you don't want to be stumbling into any of that." He directed them to the stables.

The deep rich smell of hay and manure filled Jane with memories of her grandparents. She loved to ride. While the stable hand hooked a horse to the cart, she asked, "Are we permitted to ride while we're here?"

He paused and nodded. "Of course, my lady. Any of these horses are available."

Excitement thrilled her. "Thank you."

When the cart was ready, Lord Smithy helped her up and then sat beside her, taking up the reins. "Where to, my lady?"

She loved the sound of that from his lips. As she looked out around the grounds, the creak of an old gate caught her ears. On the far side of the west gardens, it moved slightly in the wind. "Could we fit through there, do you think?" She pointed.

41

"I don't see why not. Shall we discover the mystery of the west gate?"

She laughed and held her bonnet when the wind picked up again. "We shall."

He slapped the reins, and Jane readied herself for a jolt as the horse moved forward. But the horse was slow, beyond slow. A sloth might have moved faster. Charles jiggled the reins, shouted, "Hiyah!" and jumped in his seat.

At last, the horse moved forward at a standard walking gait.

She breathed out in relief. "There's a boy. You can do it."

They finally made their way to the gate and exited onto a lovely space of ground in between the inner gardens and an outer wall. She pointed to the top of the stonework. "Do you suppose all that broken glass keeps people away?"

Lord Smithy shaded his eyes and said, "Perhaps. The wall is rather high as well. Unless one was upon a horse, I'm not sure how anyone would scale it, and then to place one's hand on the top there to get a grip . . ." He cringed. "People are better off sneaking in through the front door, honestly."

She considered his comment. Truth. The gate stood open or was guarded by a footman, maybe a pair.

They settled into a comfortable gait, the cart swaying forward and back. In the distance a crumbling old well filled the space across the center of their old donkey path. "Let's make a wish at the well."

They pulled near, and Jane was startled by a groan. "What?" She whipped her head around and hopped off the cart. A man in Regency attire sat with his head in his hands, his back up against the wall in the space between the well and the wall, his knees to his chest. She rushed to him. "Are you all right, sir?"

He groaned again and did not move. She rested a hand on his shoulder.

"Maybe back up a little bit." Lord Smithy moved forward. "Allow me?"

She nodded.

He grabbed the man by the shoulders and gave him a gentle shake. "Excuse me. Sir. Are you unwell?" He turned to Jane. "Perhaps a bit much to drink?"

"I wonder who he is. I can't tell which one from our group." His dark, thick hair fell forward over his arms, which cushioned his head.

The man groaned again. "My head. I feel as though I've been run over by a carriage."

She and Lord Smithy shared a look. *In character even when partially unconscious. Impressive.*

"Sir. Are you awake?" Something about him intrigued Jane. His hessians, worn soft leather. His breeches, his waistcoat. He had an air of authenticity about him. She recognized real period attire. And a man who would go to those measures for this reenactment was a soul mate, certainly. But passed out drunk against the wall? Maybe he was one of the actors and the costume provided by the estate?

He lifted his head, and Jane stepped backward in shock. She gasped, a hand over her mouth. "My Regency man."

"What?" Lord Smithy eyed her with disbelief. "What did you just call him? Do you know him?"

She swallowed, trying to breathe normally. "No. Not at all. He just looked so familiar." She stared at him. Absolutely similar to the man in the painting. His exact likeness if she were to guess. How could such a thing happen?

The stranger tilted his head back against the stone wall. "I think the glowing powder has stopped its madness across my brain."

Lord Smithy snorted. "Glowing powder? Been doing some forbidden substances, have we?"

The man just groaned in response.

Lord Smithy stood. "Well, I shall run to the house to get some help. Would you mind waiting here with this racehorse of ours and keeping an eye on the druggie?" His eyebrow rose in humor at his poorly placed joke.

"Yes, of course." She swallowed.

He helped her climb back into the cart. "Are you nervous? I can stay, but it's quite a run up to the house in your slippers. I don't think he's going anywhere."

"Oh, no, not at all. I'm sorry. Yes, he obviously needs some help." She forced herself to make a normal face even though she was totally freaking out inside. "I'll be fine. Go."

He left them alone, and Jane waited until he was out of sight, then she jumped back down off the cart and rushed to his side. She couldn't deny he was the identical twin of the man in her painting. She couldn't explain it besides a guess that perhaps he was related?

She spoke in a soft voice. "We're getting you some help. Lord Smithy ran to call an ambulance."

He mumbled something. Then he raised a hand to his head and opened his eyes.

Jane gasped again. Their striking blue looked right into her own. "Hello."

He swallowed. And then he smiled. His whole face lit with an inner energy. "Hello."

"They've gone to call an ambulance. Do you know what's wrong? Why you're sitting here?" She hoped he hadn't lost his memory. She hoped he wasn't really on drugs. "You're not on drugs, are you?"

He closed his eyes again. "You're not making sense, woman.

Go fetch someone without all the useless prattle who can aid me in some way."

"What!" She teetered back on her heels and then stood. "How dare you talk to me like that?"

He opened one eye again. "Are you a lady, then? My deepest apologies. We've not been introduced."

Would he insist on acting the part of the enactment? She couldn't believe how rude he sounded, as if her job were to dance attendance upon him. "Lord Smithy has gone to call an ambulance, like I said. Too bad we left our phones at the front office, or we could have called one straight away."

"Again, you're not making sense. Perhaps if you just stopped talking?" He closed his eyes again, and Jane could tell by the very still way in which he held his head that he was in considerable pain.

She decided to hold off on judging him until he felt better, but she knew one thing for sure, and that was that she might not like her Regency man after all.

# CHAPTER 6

Minutes passed, and neither he nor Lady Sullivan spoke. His head felt heavy, his eyelids wanting to close. But he kept them open, though lowered, and watched his intriguing rescuer. Her eyes were trained on the house and flitted back to him so often he wondered if her head spun. He groaned. His most certainly did.

Who was this beautiful woman behaving in such a scandalous manner? At first he thought her a servant, a brazen servant for her crass language, different manner of speaking, and incredible breach of propriety to his person. Her hand squeezed his shoulder. She spoke to him as an equal. So it only made sense that she would be a noble as well, though a poorly educated one.

Her eyes peered at him, wide, like she was seeing a ghost or some other sort of oddity. He cleared his throat. "I know it isn't usually done without a proper introduction, but since you are here at my rescue, I feel it only fitting that I know your name?"

When she didn't answer immediately, he said, "Allow me. I am Ramsbury. The Duke of Shelton."

Her eyes widened. "Do you know how long I have wanted to know your name?" Her words came out in a whisper, almost carried away on the wind. Then she shook her head. "I mean, no, that's impossible. I'm sorry." She held out her hand. "I am Lady Sullivan. Pleasure to meet you."

*Lady Sullivan.* He had never heard of such a person. And if he'd met her, he would surely have remembered such an exquisite creature, though outspoken for a woman. He wondered just how outspoken and hoped more so.

He took her hand in his own, her soft skin surprising him. Then he brought her knuckles to his lips. The feel of her skin beneath his mouth made him wish to linger, but he lowered her hand during the expected moment, his lips tingling from the touch. "You aren't wearing your gloves." He cleared his throat.

She blinked, twice, before she responded. "Oh. No. I took them off when we saw you. I'm not . . . they're so white. I suppose I should get used to them though, for the party." She waved at the house behind them.

She said such odd things. "And where did you say you are from?"

"Oh, I'm from America, the United States."

"What? But your title?" *American?* Nothing made sense. Perhaps his brain was addled. He closed his eyes. If he slept for a moment, when he awoke, the world would make sense again.

"No! Wake up."

His eyes flew open. "What is it, woman?"

"Concussion." She rested a hand on his forehead and tried to look into his eyes. "We don't know what's wrong with you yet. Stay awake."

Gibberish to him. Concussion. Her words strung together in such a strange way he was equal parts alarmed and enchanted.

"But for the purposes of the party, I'm from Devonshire."

His mind raced through Devonshire families. "Cousin to the Hamiltons?" He thought he remembered mention once of a distant Sullivan come to stay.

"Sure. That'll work. Do you know such a family?"

"I do."

"And are they a reputable choice?"

He squinted his eyes. Wouldn't she know? They were her family after all. "Of course, as you know."

Shouts came from the direction of the house. She got down beside him again. And whispered in an almost feverish way. "I don't know how or why, but this feels very important to me. Something . . . odd is going on. I hope we can get to know each other better at the party. I'm here if you need anything."

A group of men in strange white clothing with a white carried platform came running to his side.

He edged back and tried to blend in with the fence in fear, his heart pounding. "Who are they?"

"Shh. It's all right. They're here to help."

He eyed them with suspicion. "I don't think so." A young man, couldn't have been more than the duke's age of twenty-one, lifted his wrist and pressed his fingers into it.

"Unhand me." He tried to pull his hand away, but another man held him still.

"Easy there, just stay with us." He lifted Algernon's eyelid and shone a searing white light.

"Gah. Enough. How can any of you think to touch my person? Please, woman, tell them to desist as once."

"It's okay. Hold still, they're here to help. Now just cooperate for a moment so we can see if you are well."

"Of course I'm not well. Do I look well?"

And then his host, the woman he'd supped with only this evening, approached with a cup of tea. "Excuse me, let me through."

"You. Praises. I've met the strangest individuals. Is this part of my journey?"

Her eyes twinkled at him. "It is." She crouched down to his front. "Tea, Your Grace?"

Of all the ridiculous notions. "No, I do not want tea."

"Miss. I can't have you giving the patient any substances." The paramedic gently nudged her to move out of the way.

"Oh tosh. What harm could there be in a bit of tea? It's meant to calm him, isn't it? Do take a sip, Your Grace. It will help with what ails you."

Something in her eyes eased his hesitation, so he reached for the cup, but as he raised it to his lips, she watched with such an unnerving intensity, he touched his mouth to it only and then tossed its contents onto the ground beside him. "I find I am not desiring tea at the moment, after all."

Nellie's eyes flashed, but she shrugged delicately and said, "As you wish."

The men lifted him under the shoulders and at his feet and carried him to the white platform. "What is this? I do not wish to be handled in such a way."

"Let us get you to the ambulance." They pulled strong white tethers across him and imprisoned him flat.

He struggled and squirmed, he twisted. "Let me free. I demand to be left alone at once."

The men ran with him to the front drive, and nothing he could do would free his arms or legs from their carry. The

49

woman ran at his side, Lady Sullivan. "Do be still Your Grace. You are creating quite a stir."

At last she spoke a sentence he could follow. "Tell them I do not wish for treatment."

The men stopped in front of the house, and another one came forward. "Are you declining our services?"

"Yes, I am. I've been trying to decline them for some time."

"Understood." The man who seemed to be in charge conferred with the others. "His vitals are good." Then he turned to Algernon with a stiff board and a piece of paper. "Could you please sign here? And here?" He held out a blue stickish sort of device that when Algernon placed it on the paper made marks. Astounded, he wrote his name where indicated.

"Excellent." The straps fell away from his legs, and he rotated his arms. "I do believe I'd like to keep this device, if you don't mind . . ." He held up the writing stick.

"Our pen?" The man shrugged. "Sure. It's yours. You're probably going to pay for it anyway." He smirked and motioned for the men to follow him. They helped Algernon to his feet and then took the carry bed and entered a boxy shiny metallic carriage with black small wheels and drove off at incredible speeds.

"I am astounded." He turned to Lady Sullivan. "Have you ever seen the like?"

Her eyes looked troubled, unsure. "Well, I—"

His hostess clapped her hands. "Now that all these terribly modern conveyances have left, our house party can begin. Welcome to 1817!"

A maid approached with another cup of tea. She curtsied before him and held it out. Confound it. This woman and her tea.

"Your Grace. This tea is our household brew. You will find it restorative."

His head ached and the world seemed a bit out of place, so he nodded, sipped a tiny swallow, and found it delicious, the perfect temperature and comforting in an odd way, so he tipped back the cup and drank the remaining contents in one swallow. "Capital! A delicious cup of tea."

A warmth filled him, and his worry decreased. The lingering pain in his head went away, and suddenly, everything made sense. Even if it didn't make sense, it made sense. The men all around him earlier, wearing absurd clothes, made sense. They were the doctors, of course.

His hostess nodded. "I do believe he's well." She leaned closer. "How do you feel?"

He waved his arms around, felt his head. "She's right. I feel magnificent. Better than I have in years."

Lady Sullivan looked at their hostess and back at him. "Are you sure you're all right? I think you might need to go get checked out just to be sure."

"No, he's fine." Their hostess looked at him. "You're fine, aren't you?"

He moved his head around and clapped his hands. "I feel better than ever." He offered Lady Sullivan his arm. "Now, if you'll accompany me into the house, I would like some more of that tea, if you don't mind." He nodded to the woman. Was she the housekeeper? Who was this woman? He stopped. "Excuse me, but might you and I be introduced, officially?"

"Oh, how strange. We never did take care of that formality, did we?" She held out her hand. "You will know me here as Nellie, the housekeeper."

That was rather untoward, the housekeeper going by her first name, but again, somehow it made sense in his mind. Of course she would. "Pleased to meet you. Ramsbury, the Duke of Shelton."

She nodded and then moved to talk to the men in the strange clothing. He turned to the lovely woman on his arm who he found less odd and more charming the longer he breathed. "Shall we, Lady Sullivan?"

She nodded, her eyes wide. "If you're certain. You really did not look well when we found you."

Nellie waved them inside. "He'll be well in just a few moments." She clapped her hands. "Let the party begin!"

As they stepped into the house, Lady Sullivan's hand applied pressure to his forearm. "I'm rather excited about the time we have. I'm here for research purposes, somewhat of an expert on this topic, but I hope to add some unique research in my dissertation."

Why was she whispering? He placed his hand over top of her bare one. "I, too, am happy to be here, especially to make your acquaintance." The chandelier caught his eye. "What in the blazes!"

Lady Sullivan stopped. "What?" She followed his gaze up to the ceiling.

The room shimmered in his vision and then the light coming from the chandelier made sense. Even though it came not from flickering candles but from some sort of perpetually burning glow. He would need to study it further for when he returned. He wanted just such a light in his own home.

They rounded a corner. A woman stood on the stairs' landing scantily clothed. He held a hand to his heart in shock. He was horrified and fascinated all at the same time. A woman was waving her hands around and looked to be directing a trunk up the stairs. But clothed in the strangest underclothing he had ever imagined. A bit of shirt stretched tight across her top, her stomach and navel bare for all to see. He, of course, was not versed in women's underclothing, but he had seen it at a milliner a time or two. But these clothes he had never seen the like. The full length of her legs was stretched out in front of him with the smallest bit of fabric tight around her hips. "Good heavens, I do apologize." He turned immediately about so that his back was to her person.

She giggled. The woman on the stairs, instead of being horrified at being caught in such a life-changing scandalous disadvantage, found their situation amusing. He looked to Lady Sullivan, who eyed him with a great amount of amusement as well and a tiny spark of something. He looked closer. Respect. Ah, so she appreciated good breeding. Well, thank heavens for that.

He spoke through his teeth. "Has she gone?"

She shook her head. "I'm afraid not." She cleared her throat and indicated with her head that someone approached.

*Surely not.* A hand tapped his shoulder. "Pardon me. I did not mean to be so casually dressed. I had a bit of a car, ahem, carriage mishap and am woefully unprepared for my first day. I will remedy the problem immediately."

He nodded.

"Before I go, might we be introduced?"

He widened his eyes and looked to Lady Sullivan. She shrugged. He shook his head. Then he said, "Since neither of us has made your acquaintance prior and you are most unsuitably attired, I shall wait until tea for the pleasure of an introduction."

Silence followed and perhaps a tiny huff. The sound of soft footsteps and multiple creaks sounded until silence again filled the hall.

He peeked over his shoulder. "I assume she's gone?"

"Yes, quite." Then Lady Sullivan giggled. "Oh my."

"Oh my indeed. I find nothing about that whole inter-change amusing. Perhaps her brain is addled. Coming out here with almost nothing on." He cleared his throat. "She could be ruined. And me, strapped to her side forever because of it. Nothing amusing that I can see, no." He expected women to resort to drastic measures to ensnare him as a husband. But this was the most untoward attempt he had yet encountered.

He had not yet turned to face the stairs fully, afraid she might return. They stood in the front entry, where he had first met Nellie. It looked the same and yet different, much older and yet cleaner. He couldn't describe the difference. Perhaps it was also the addition of greater illumination from the extraordinary chandelier.

The front door opened and two gentlemen entered followed by two more ladies. They chattered together in such an open familiarity, Ramsbury felt sure they must be family. The ladies were lovely, the men seemed jovial. And of the larger stature, like himself.

They approached, and the first man, dark hair, curly, held out a hand. "I'm Todd. I don't remember seeing you on the page. New?" He smiled and Ramsbury could make no sense of what he was saying.

"Pardon me? Todd? Is that your name?"

"In character already, are you? Or are you staff?" He looked from Lady Sullivan to himself as if to solve a mystery.

Affronted, Algernon wondered what about his person gave this man the impression he was a servant. "I'm most certainly not the staff. Ramsbury, Duke of Shelton." He nodded to the man. That should put him more in his place. What did he mean, throwing out first names?

The women in his party stared with wide eyes and then

curtsied.

This Todd person swallowed, something competitive flashed in his eyes and then he bowed. "Lord Engel, at your service. And this is Lord Tinder and Ladies Billings and Farrow." He looked to Lady Sullivan with raised eyebrows.

Ramsbury searched her face. He was loath to share her with anyone else, but of course he must. "And this is Lady Sullivan of Devonshire." She curtsied, and the man bowed over her hand, lingering in a ridiculous fashion.

He cleared his throat. "We were just going to see about some tea, if you'd care to join us?"

The ladies looked to one another. Everyone in the group behaved in such a strange manner. Perhaps he and Lady Sullivan should continue without them. He made a move to turn them toward the front parlor.

Another voice called from behind them. "Lady Sullivan. There you are."

She removed her hand from his arm, and he felt the loss of it immediately. A man approached. As he bowed, Ramsbury recognized him as the one who had first awakened him at the wall.

Lady Sullivan introduced them, and then Lord Smithy reached for her hand and placed it on his arm.

Ramsbury burned with irritation.

But Lord Smithy ignored his glares. With eyes only for Lady Sullivan, he led her away. "Shall we finish our walk?"

She turned to him with apology in her expression but moved rather quickly off with the new Lord Smithy as though tea with Ramsbury were inconsequential.

Except in the rare moments he and his father were in the same room, Ramsbury couldn't recall another time he had felt inconsequential.

# CHAPTER 7

*J*ane sipped from her lemonade at dinner. She suspected it wasn't quite as watered down as the Regency version was purported to be, because hers was delicious, just sweet enough, just tart enough.

At her side Lord Smithy winked and grinned. "I heard that you ladies have something nefarious planned."

She raised an eyebrow. "Nefarious?" His toe nudged hers. "Yes. We do. We shall discuss it after dinner in the front parlor, with you gentlemen none the wiser."

"Oh, but we are on to your plans and have an equally scandalous idea ourselves."

She gasped. "Surely not."

"Forgive me. Scandalous was perhaps not the correct word to use. Perhaps just a touch risky? And sinfully innocent?"

The ladies around the table giggled. And His Grace frowned. He sat across from her, and every time she looked in his direction, he was staring into her face. Brooding. It made him more appealing for some reason, his dark blue eyes pulling her in. She had not been able to speak with him alone since yesterday, and she longed for an opportunity to show him the painting in her book. His likeness was so much the same as the person in the painting's, he must be a relation. She hoped he could shed some light on it whatever the case. She sensed he would have answers to all her questions, that he could open even the mysteries of her soul if she let him. She shook her head. She tended to overdramatize matters of the heart. But the very twin of her Regency hero showing up at an enactment party during the two weeks when she hoped to unveil the painting's secrets seemed far too aligned to be coincidental.

Lady Farrow, sitting at the duke's side, rested her hand on his arm. "I think we should have a dance this evening, in the back parlor."

Oh no she didn't. No one laid claim on her Regency man before she did. "I agree." They turned to Nellie, their hostess-turned-housekeeper, who curtsied. "Of course. We can roll back the rugs after games in the parlor this evening."

Lord Smithy lifted her hand to his lips. "Might I have the first set?"

"And I the second," His Grace demanded from across the table. Suddenly she was not as amused by the manly grappling for her time. She did have a say and was about to exercise her independence when Lord Smithy shook his head, slightly, and she remembered she had a part to play. How would a Regency woman respond? But wasn't this the very thing she was trying to prove in her dissertation? Women of all sorts of personalities were present in 1817. So in this moment, a woman like her, a woman like the character of Elizabeth Bennet, how would she respond? There were plenty of examples in literature, more or less, but in real life? Now.

She grappled with a manner in which to express herself. "I

should be happy to respond to a request for my time when it is accomplished in a gentlemanly manner."

The ladies sucked in their breath, and the duke changed color. He didn't go precisely white, but he did look as though he worked to control himself. Then he snorted and started shaking. And the other members of the table looked on in shock. Lady Farrow at his side rested a hand on his arm again. "Are you quite all right, Your Grace?"

Then his face broke into a grin. And he breathed in a great breath of air in between heaving laughs. "At last. Well done."

"I beg your pardon?" Jane wasn't sure how to respond because His Grace wasn't precisely sticking to a known manner in which to address others at a dinner party.

"At last someone with the nerve to stand up to my nonsense." His face relaxed into such a joyful look of ease and expression, it made him that much more handsome. And she found herself without words.

He bowed his head. "I do apologize for my earlier manner in addressing you. Lady Sullivan, would you do me the great honor of saving the second and third sets for me this evening? I find I am in need of your excellent company, and though I know it is in high demand, I wish for the smallest portion of it." His eyes, filled with earnest hope, and his face, deferential— she had never felt more honored by a petition.

"Pon rep, I've never received so gallant an invitation. Yes, thank you. I would be delighted to spend the time with you."

He nodded and resumed eating.

The others at the table began talking among themselves in hushed tones. Lord Smithy was silent at her side. Then he leaned closer and whispered. "Is he for real? Because if he's not staff, *he* is our competition."

She studied His Grace with new eyes. Could he be a staff member, spying on them? Someone as dedicated as she to the intricacies of Regency social etiquette? Either way, she looked forward to finding out more during their sets. Two with the handsome duke. She tried to swallow her excitement but was unsuccessful and instead choked on a piece of fish.

They separated after dinner, the men taking their port, or whatever the party provided, and the women gathering in the sitting room. She marveled at the activities offered. A half-finished needlepoint waited at one chair, a stack of books adorned at a small table, a pianoforte stood in the corner, many chairs awaited conversation in small groupings. Jane was charmed by it all. And if it weren't so tedious, she longed to try needlepoint. Perhaps in the late afternoon hours she would add a few stitches.

As soon as the door was closed, Lady Farrow huffed. "Did you hear His Grace's petition?" She whipped around to Lady Sullivan. "I don't think it quite fair that two men are giving attention to just one of the ladies. Isn't the idea that we all pair off?"

A maid in the corner looked their way.

So Jane wandered over to the books. "I don't know. At any other house party I've been to, the numbers are equal, men and women, but we all spend time with who we wish to in the moment. I'm certain attention will rotate and change as the time goes on."

"Oh stop. The men aren't even here. We don't need to be in character all the time."

Lady Billings joined Jane at the books. "What are you reading?"

"Oh, a fellow reader? There is a remarkably well-kept copy

of *Pride and Prejudice*. Though as it was published only four years ago, it doesn't seem to be as well read as I would expect."

"I love that book."

Jane opened it to the first page to check date of publication. The typeset, the binding, the whole layout of the book seemed to date it in its original publication. But often publishers would re-create that effect to sell more books. As she examined the front page of the crisp new pages, she nearly dropped the book. "Look!" Her hands started shaking. *Impossible.* "This says this book is from the original printing. But how can that be?" She swallowed. Looking up, her eyes found Nellie. The woman watched her for a moment and then winked.

What on earth was going on? Surely it was a facsimile. But she checked the markings, the ink set, even the type of ink and its bleed on the paper. This counterfeit was done by an expert. A counterfeit certainly, or an original kept in a vacuum for all these years. For the first time in her life, she wished to pilfer someone's property. When she returned the book to the table, she touched it two more times before walking away and leaving it.

The evening passed quickly. Jane and Lord Smithy beat everyone they played in whist, His Grace growing more irritated every hand they played, and then the carpets were rolled back and a maid called upon to play the pianoforte for them.

Jane knew it highly unlikely a maid during the Regency era would have had the ability to play, but she kept quiet since she most looked forward to dancing all the dances of the era.

The music began, and everyone paired up and stood in a line. Lord Smithy faced her with an open grin, which she returned.

They began the steps. Jane had participated in local dancing and in small reenactments for years. She had taken hours of lessons and worked hard in practice, watching YouTube channel videos. So she felt pretty proficient—if not expert, she at least didn't expect to step on toes.

But when the duke danced, she struggled to keep up. His feet moved effortlessly, he participated in droll conversation, he made them all laugh as he circled about through each lady in turn and then threw in extra moves none of them had ever seen.

When the music stopped and they had a small break before the second set, he approached. "You do these differently than I have ever seen, and you all do the same steps together. Where did you learn?"

"From our dance instructors, of course." Jane looked around, aware of many eyes watching.

"And I as well, but my instructors and those of everyone else I've ever seen instructed me differently. Curious."

They were called for another round of dancing. Twelve couples lined up. The duke stepped forward. "I'm not really all that accomplished at dancing."

"You're the best I've ever seen." Jane felt her face heat at her own exuberance, but she looked forward to dancing with him, in fact wished to do so every day they were at the house party. Perhaps she could learn his particular dances and practice with him.

As he passed her, he said, "Perhaps this might seem too soon to say, but I wish to know you better, to spend many hours dancing thus."

She grinned overly large before she could stop herself but had time to compose her next sentence as they circled, before he returned. "I too desire such a thing. From the moment I met you I've been intrigued." She moved past. Then panicked.

Royally freaked out. Had she said too much? Was that too forward? What would he think?

But when he circled back, his face was open, sincere. "Then I am not alone in my fascinations." He dipped his head. "Perhaps we could spend some time in the library tomorrow."

She moved down the line in the arms of Lord Smithy. He quirked an eyebrow. "Genius. Keep the competition close." Then he winked and passed her off to the next man, who got the benefit of her rolled eyes. *Oops.* They didn't roll eyes back then.

When she was at last with the duke again, she said, "I'd like nothing more. Perhaps during a free moment?"

The dance ended and everyone clapped. The duke stayed nearby because they were to dance another. The music to a waltz began, and with a grin she didn't bother to dim, she stepped into his arms.

He placed his hand on the small of her back, and she felt its heat through her dress and stays. Or she imagined it, but with his large pressure there, she found it difficult to concentrate. Then he lifted her hand in his own and held it out to their side. "You are closer than I usually hold a woman." His voice had turned husky, his eyes dark.

For a moment, she was frozen by the deep blue of his eyes, searching for meaning in her face. She stammered. "I'm sorry. Should I step away?"

"No, no. I see others are the same. It must be more your custom here, again. So strange. But I'm pleased. I'd not like to lose your closeness."

"Nor I yours." She stepped closer. "I like pushing boundaries."

He wrapped his hand around her to feel her close. "I don't know what you mean by this pushing of boundaries, but I can guess and, in this case, fully agree. Where I'm from, some say I'm a bit of a rogue."

"Do they?" Her interest piqued, she wanted to know everything about him.

"Yes, and many say I am uncouth." He watched her.

"So far I've seen only a touch of the rogue—I like a little rogue in a man—and nothing of the uncouth. You've been only a gentleman."

He watched her a moment. "And you like that about me, that I'm a gentleman."

"Most certainly."

"Are not all men of your acquaintance gentlemen? Certainly as a lady, most men you associate with are."

"Gentlemen are as gentlemen do and say. It is far more than a title."

He stopped. "That is perhaps the most profound thing I've ever heard a lady say."

She felt her face heat. "Thank you."

His nearness, his musky smell, his strong arms circling her, she knew why some thought the waltz a scandalous dance. The longer they danced, the closer she wanted to be and found herself watching his mouth more often than she had any other man's.

As their dance neared its end, he whispered. "I am overcome. Are you feeling as I, with a wish for some fresh air?"

She swallowed. And nodded. Was this the Regency way to ask if she wanted to make out? Then yes! But she couldn't be sure.

He placed her hand in the crook of his elbow and led them out the side door into a small garden. It was lit by candles and torches. Benches offered a choice of places to sit and paths to walk on. The cool night air felt nice on her arms and neck. "Oh this is lovely. Thank you."

He kept her hand on his arm, leading them down the first path. "Might I speak freely?"

"Yes. I would like that."

"I've never been so moved by a woman."

His eyes were so intense. His voice sincere, his language still in character. What was she to think? Was this part of their act or was he telling her he was interested? She said, "Your words thrill me. I can hardly breathe, but I wonder at your sincerity since we've only just met."

"Again you challenge me." His eyes lit with pure enjoyment. "Do you have any idea how pleasurable it is for me to have a woman challenge me?"

She squeezed his arm. "Then you and I will get along just fine. I find I challenge most people in one way or another."

"You say the strangest things, in a manner I am not accustomed to hearing."

"What? Really? Do I not sound correct?"

"Correct? Certainly. You just have a delightful and refreshing uniqueness about you."

She nodded, not sure what to think. She guessed he was complimenting her, but she had never received such a compliment or spent time with such a man. In fact, all her Regency dreams were coming true all in one night. "Have you ever had your likeness painted?"

She was dying to know. Was it him? His relation, rather?

"Yes, countless times. I tire of the exercise."

"I'd imagine so, if that's the case." She walked a few more steps. "I am thinking of one painting in particular. Might I bring you a book to look at in the library tomorrow?"

"Certainly. I look forward to it. Does this book have a particular drawing in it you'd like me to see?"

"Yes, a painting."

They arrived at a fountain in the center of the garden. "I'd love to see anything you'd care to show me." He stepped in front of her, the moon shining above them, lighting his eyes in the darkness. "Lady Sullivan."

"Call me Jane."

"Jane." His voice caressed her name as though it were precious. She wanted to beg him to say it again. Then he did. "Jane." His hands ran up her arms and across her back, pulling her closer. "I am overcome. I want nothing more than to press my lips to yours, but we are not acquainted nearly enough."

"Or perhaps more than enough." His hand at her upper back, teasing her bare skin, his nearness, his deep voice sending tremors through her. Nearly overcome herself, she stepped closer and lifted her chin.

His lips were close, a breath away. He whispered. "I would love to kiss you."

She lifted herself up on her toes and closed the distance between their mouths. "I'm right here." Her lips brushed his as she spoke. She hadn't meant to, but he tilted his head, making it a natural consequence. Tingles rushed through her, and she thrilled at his nearness.

He closed his eyes. "But we must wait."

Then he stepped back, leaving her breath coming heavy and her heart pounding with yearning. "What?"

"We must wait until we are sure. You have no chaperone here. I have no one to talk to or to make my intentions known. I would be the utmost cad if I were to take advantage." He wiped his brow and cleared his throat. "Though I find you difficult to resist."

She almost threw herself back in his arms, proclaiming, *I like cads*, but resisted. Something about his gesture, his nobility, even if he was playing a character, impressed her, and his forbearance made her feel special, precious, cared for.

So she placed her hand on his arm and tried to calm her pounding heart.

"You have made it difficult to clear my thoughts." He grinned at her out of the side of his eye. "No woman has ever distracted me so."

"You say the most beautiful things. I hope some of what you are saying is real, that it's not all just some act, because I would like to get to know you, to be with you, even after these two weeks?" How desperate did she sound? Wasn't he supposed to make the next move? She didn't know. The rules of dating seemed forced and awkward to her, and she didn't want to wait. She wanted him now.

"I give you my word, I mean everything I say to you."

She nodded, trying to believe. "Thank you."

When they entered in through the door, the room had emptied and the house felt quiet. "Oh dear. They've all gone up to bed." Jane wondered what the other guests thought of their disappearance, what Lord Smithy thought.

They tiptoed quietly through the hallways and up the stairs. "Your Grace."

"Call me Algernon, but only in private. I'll save Jane for our private conversations as well."

"Algernon."

"Hmm?"

"Thank you."

He pulled her close in the dark, an embrace full of the sweetness of unfulfilled yearning. "Until tomorrow, then."

She nodded up against his broad chest. "Tomorrow."

He left her at her door. When she closed it upon entering her room, she leaned up against the frame and closed her eyes.

"That terrible?"

Her breath caught. "What? Who's there?"

A match lit and then a candle. Lord Smithy. He eyed her, his face full of humor. "Or was it that good?"

# CHAPTER 8

*J*ane looked around for her maid in alarm. "Stop that. What are you doing in here?"

"I'm doing what they all did at house parties, sneaking around during the night."

She laughed, but felt a sudden disloyalty to Algernon, to their time together.

His eyes widened in mock innocence. "I thought we could compare notes."

Ah, for research. She could do that. She moved to sit at her table. "Come sit." She waved him over.

He did, but moved his chair as close as he could to hers, facing her, leaning forward so that their knees touched and their breath almost mingled. He lit a candle, his handsome features more striking in the flickering mellow glow. "I've learned some more details about this contest." He spoke quietly, his voice barely above a murmur. She leaned closer to him, his cologne filling the air between them.

"How are you hearing these things? I've yet to hear anything at all."

"If they told all the guests, no one would slip up, would they?"

She nodded. "True. And you know because?"

"I have a friend on the inside. One of the maids."

She didn't want to know if it were her Dorothy. Something about that felt like an infringement of her privacy, but she didn't know why. It's not like he was spying on her. He was just getting intel about the contest from the maid.

She had planned to ask for access to all the documents, to the paintings, to any old artifacts in the home while she was here. When she called them about it months ago, they had told her to ask again once she had completed the party. The owners of the items were unusually selective about who could see them. Few in the world had ever had the chance and no one had touched them outside the circle of owners. But Jane felt it was time for the letters to be read, before they became so old they were illegible. A concern tickled at her peace. But perhaps they had put her off before because they had this contest in mind already, their quirky way of choosing only those who were worthy of the time period?

"Why do you want to see their artifacts?"

He paused, then searched her face, the candlelight flickering in his eyes. "I am most interested in the women who lived there, their personalities, lives, reactions to things."

Jane's heart picked up.

"And in one particular duke."

Curious, she wanted to know more. "Was he a relation?"

"No, but he possibly could have been. I have reason to believe he might have been courting one of the daughters. That he was connected to their house in some way."

Jane's breathing picked up. "None of the sisters ever

married . . . or so people say. Why would they never have married?"

His eyes lit with excitement. "You don't believe it."

"No, do you?"

"No, I just don't think women were capable of making their way on their own. For them to have lived as long as some of them did, for there to be records at all, at least one man had to be involved." He continued talking in hushed excited tones, but Jane's ears pounded and her vision blurred in her anger. Of course they were capable.

Once he'd finally exhausted all his unsubstantiated and irritating theories about the weakness of women in the Regency time period, she said, "My theory is based on facts much simpler. I don't believe they stayed single, because if they had, they would have stayed in the house. It wasn't entailed."

He stopped and frowned. "True." Then he held up a finger, and she wanted to warn him to not even continue. "Unless you consider that they weren't capable of running a household and taking care of the tenants and handling the income and books and things . . ."

She shook her head. "Of all the ridiculous—"

A soft tap stopped her tirade. "Jane." The duke's voice whispered through her door.

"Oh no." Jane wished to hide.

Lord Smithy's eyebrows raised in surprise and appreciation. "Dalliances with two men in one night?"

"Charles, stop." She used his first name on purpose to talk some sense in him. "I don't want anyone to see any men in my room at a Regency reenactment. This is enough to get me ruined, twice, and married to one of you."

He ran a hand from her shoulder to her fingertips. "I had

hoped to give you even a small reason to consider a little Regency ruination this evening."

"What about our contest?"

"Well, no one would know, would they?"

The duke tapped again; then the doorknob turned.

"What!" Jane whispered. "Out on the balcony!" She shoved Charles, Lord Smithy, away and leaped to grab a robe to wrap around herself. Her gown hung off her shoulder and had seemed fine in a room full of people, but in her bedroom felt more like a negligée or something, a floor-length negligée. She laughed to herself. She didn't know why, but she was much more conscious of appearing appropriately dressed in front of Algernon than Charles, likely influenced by the earlier freak-out moment with the girl in the shorts. She laughed, thinking about it, and then pulled the slowly opening door all the way back.

The duke straightened from his bent and sneaking position and smiled. His cravat was loosened, a button undone, and he wore no jacket. But his breeches were still gloriously hugging his thighs. He was a delicious man in any circumstance. And their almost kiss still burned her lips whenever she thought about it.

His eyes sharpened, and he looked up over her head. "Is there someone on your balcony? Stay back. I'll take a look."

"Oh, no, no, um it's just, uh . . ." She could think of nothing to say.

He moved to the doors, opened them and then stepped outside. She didn't even follow, the moonlight lighting what area she did see.

After a quick peek, he returned shaking his head. "Must have been my mind imagining up a man waiting for his good-night kiss."

She coughed. "No, nothing like that here. Although . . ." She stepped closer, ready to tease him. "What are *you* doing here in the middle of the night?"

He stepped back. "No, it's nothing like that."

She raised her eyebrows.

"Well, maybe it's a little bit like that." He ran a hand through his hair. "I couldn't sleep."

She shut the door behind them and lit another candle, which she handed to him. "This is excellent, because there's a book I've been wanting you to see."

He craned his head to the shut door. "Are you sure this is wise? The door. Wait, a book? You want to . . . read?"

"Yes, of course. You will also when you see."

He shook his head.

"Now sit. I'll be just a minute." She rushed into her closet, amazed at the organization of her maid. Everything was put in its place and clothes for tomorrow already set out and pressed. She dug around her trunk and pulled out her book on artwork from the Regency era.

A thrilling feeling of expectation pounded through her as she rushed back to Algernon's side. Her hands shook as she sat beside him, and the book fell open to her well-worn page.

"Why, that's me! But I don't recall ever sitting for this, or anyone watching at Almack's." He frowned. "This looks to be in Almack's, doesn't it?" He peered closer. "But how did its likeness come to be in a book?" He closed the cover, examining. "Who was able to do such a remarkable thing?" He opened the front page. "2009!" He dropped it. Then his eyes flicked up to hers. They were filled with fear.

"What? What is it, Algernon?" She didn't know how to help him. His fear seemed uncharacteristic and misplaced.

"How can this be?" He blinked several times and then seemed to relax. "I feel better, but this still makes no sense to me. It's as if my mind is allowing it to be true even though it cannot be."

Jane felt more and more confused. "You aren't making sense."

"I don't suppose I am, but neither are you, if you want to know the truth. Nothing about most of this should be making sense. I stopped by the kitchen. What manner of machinery is all of that?" His earnest eyes bored into hers. "Something about this house and the woman who seems to run it is not right."

She cleared her throat. "Let's start with the book, shall we? The rest is too much to process right now."

"Process, sometimes you speak such strange words and then other times you sound just like the ladies back home." His eyes squinted at her in the candlelight as if trying to understand.

She tried to control her breathing, suspecting something that couldn't possibly be true. *One thing at a time.* "You . . . you said this picture is you?" She pointed to her Regency man. The one she had been obsessing over for years.

"Yes, you see yourself, the likeness. It looks incredibly well done. And this woman is Lady Anna, a dear friend. I visited this past summer. Family of women, lovely sisters. But I don't remember ever commissioning this work or seeing it anywhere besides right now in your book."

"And they painted your likeness?"

"I presume so. I don't know who did such a thing. As you can see. Now tell me how it came to be in a book such as this?" He flipped to the copyright page. "And this date? Is this the date?"

73

"Well, it's ten years ago, but yes, it's accurate."

He sat back, his expression deeply troubled. She wasn't sure what to say or do for him. And she began to feel a bit alarmed herself. "Is everything all right, Algernon?"

"That would mean, according to you and this book, it's 2019." He studied the book's copyright page. "No. I should not be fine. But I feel perfectly normal. I am puzzled, but as soon as I might begin to feel agitated, my brain just accepts the new knowledge. It happens to me multiple times in a day." He sat forward again. "It's that Nellie woman."

"She is a bit . . . odd. But tell me what disturbs you."

"To begin, there are no chamber pots."

"Thank heavens for that." She laughed, but then noticed he was serious. "You prefer chamber pots to a toilet?"

"No, I didn't know anything about a toilet until my valet went in to use one and . . . I deduced their function."

Jane frowned. She couldn't understand. "And this image is you?"

"Yes."

So many things to consider, but for some reason, the one thing most on her mind came out of her lips first. "Can you tell me what you are so smug about?"

"What?"

"I've been wondering for years why you are smiling. I can't believe you are right here and I can ask you." She stopped. Of course this image couldn't really be Algernon. The man was living in some kind of other mental reality. There must be a diagnosis for it. What are the odds that the very image she obsesses over would be the same one he displaced himself into?

"How could you be wondering for years when I appear

about the same age as I am now? And you still haven't answered any of my questions about why it is in a book."

She stilled. "So what year do you think it is?"

"1817."

She scooted back from him. Hearing him say the very year the painting was commissioned somehow made everything a touch more real. "A picture of this painting was taken, and then the digital image was added to the manuscript of this book, then it was printed."

He waved a hand in her direction. "That means nothing to me, gibberish, everything you just said."

"Algernon. What would you say if I told you the year is really 2019?"

He stood up. "I'd refuse to believe it, and then"—he blinked —"my mind tells me it makes sense." He walked out toward the balcony. "It's as if my mind's been bewitched."

He paced back and forth. "At the wall, this dust, glowing dust, fell around me and a giggling woman at the top . . . Then I fell asleep against the wall, and the next thing I knew, you came. Nothing has been the same ever since." He reached for her hands. "Do you think I've been bewitched?"

She moved him back to the table to sit down. "I don't know why you think you are living in 1817. That's the problem, isn't it? You think you are from the year 1817?"

"I *am* from the year 1817. I proved it just now with this painting."

She had to give it to him. And he was on to something. "Okay, how about a few more proofs." She thought for a moment. What could she ask him that few people knew? She ran back to her trunk and got out her almanacs. "What was the weather here three days ago?"

"Raining like crazy. Sheets of rain."

She flipped through the pages. "Correct. All night?"

"No, full moon, few clouds, as if the rain disappeared all at once."

"Correct." That was uncanny. She flipped through a few more pages. "What horse won the races a week past?"

"I don't follow horse races. Gambling was my father's downfall."

She ran for her copy of Debrett's and her printed parliamentary proceedings. "Who is your father?"

"He was the late Duke of Shelton, Ramsbury himself."

She opened up her book. "What was something he argued or voted on in the House of Lords?"

He thought for a moment. "You have to know, my father never talked to me, ever. And I stopped trying to follow him or listen to what he did."

"Was your family ever gossiped over? Written up in a cartoon or satire?"

"All the time. I and my friends are shocking to some of the more stodgy matrons. You'll find a month-long stretch of cartoons last school break when we played practical jokes at Almack's. They tried to kick me out, but since I inherited my title, they're stuck with me."

She flipped through her news journals. And sure enough, a month-long tribute to his practical jokes. She snorted. "You put vinegar in the punch?"

He shrugged. "Naturally. Their pinched faces bother me, so I thought to enhance them, make a spectacle of the pinched lips."

Jane sat back in her seat. Could he be so delusional that he had studied these minute details about his life in an effort to assume a new identity?

"If we can get to the Lichfield estate, I can prove to you that I am indeed living in 1817."

"Well, I think you must know you are not living in 1817 any longer."

"We can discuss that next. I feel it of the utmost importance to me personally that you understand."

"Okay, how can you prove it?"

"What is this o-kay? Everyone says it all the time. Is it a form of agreement?"

She eyed him. The historian in her had already noted that his reactions to most everything at the party were one hundred percent historically accurate. Up until this moment, she had just assumed he was incredibly well researched and a marvelous actor. "So how can you prove it?"

"We must go there."

"Excellent." She stood, grabbing a long coat.

"What? Where are you going?"

"We'll go there now, before everyone else wakes up."

"It must be three miles in the dark and cold. How can we accomplish such a thing?"

"I'll just call an Uber."

"Pardon me?" His confusion was genuine. She started to believe him, that her Regency man was in fact here, from 1817. And as soon as she started to admit that, she accepted the fact that she might also be going crazy.

"Never mind. You're just gonna have to trust me and follow along."

She dug through her trunk again for a flashlight, and they headed out down the hallway. In the house, they used candles to light the way in case they were spotted. She still wanted to maintain her spot as most historically accurate person at the party. They slipped out the front door and made their way down the long drive on foot.

"Will we be walking?"

"No, just trust me."

The lights of their Uber came toward them down the road, and Algernon held a hand up to his face. She didn't bother to reassure him. He was in for one shock after another if he persisted in the belief that he didn't live in 2019. She opened the door and gently pushed him in, then followed after. "Carriages of 2019."

He didn't answer.

She gave the driver directions to the nearby estate. When the car pulled out, he gripped at the seat in shock. Then sat forward, staring out the front window and then the side as if he'd never been in a moving car. He said nothing, but now and then rubbed his palms on the front of his breeches.

When they stood at the entry to the property, she said, "Ok —er. Right. We're here." She was secretly thrilled with what she might learn from him. Delusional or not, he knew his stuff. And this, of course, was the very house she had hoped to explore at the end of the party.

He walked forward. "There are two things I can show you that will give you undeniable proof of my existence in the year 1817. The first is outside, so let's go there where we won't have to disturb the household." He walked down the front drive, and she followed down the side of the house and through the back, over a large expanse of grass.

"Their grounds are different, but I hope that what I can show you will still be present."

They continued their walk in silence. Then he cleared his throat. "You have to know what I am about to show you doesn't portray me in the most favorable light. I am a bit of a cad. I'll admit it. But mostly I just try to avoid having to clean up the problems on my estate. I'm so ashamed of the manner in which my father managed things and I can't bring myself to fix them."

"And so you continue as he did? In mismanagement?"

He was silent for so long she thought he would ignore her question. Then he said, "I hadn't thought of it that way."

They entered a grove of trees at the back of the lawn, and she flipped on her flashlight.

He startled, then shook his head. "I should just try to stop being alarmed at every shocking thing you show me."

The path grew narrower, the trees older, and then they came to what looked to her like a pile of old stone.

"It doesn't look like much. Let's hope it's still here." He led her back behind the stone to an old tree. It looked like it might fall over any moment, but in the base of the tree was a dark, hollowed-out portion. He knelt in the soft earth.

"Wait. Use the light. Who knows what critters have come to live there in all this time." Was she believing his story? She almost was. Everything he said rang so true, and here they were in an ancient-looking place.

He reached in, pulling out piles of leaves and sticks and grappled around. Then he pulled his hand out and slumped his shoulders. "It's not there."

"Keep trying. It's been, what, two hundred years?" Two hundred and two. She'd done the math.

He shrugged.

She knelt beside him and reached her hand in, digging down in the earth at the back. She scooped out handfuls of the soft, barky earth until she'd made quite an indent at the base of the inside of the tree, and then her fingers felt something hard. "I've got something." The thrill of a mystery filled her. She hoped it was all true, at the same time not knowing how it possibly could be.

He nudged her aside and reached in, busily moving his arm about in a feverish fashion. Until he pulled out a box the size of his hand.

"And here is my proof."

She moved closer, shining the light on the box.

"I'm going to tell you exactly what's in this box. Before I do, take a good look. Does it appear to have been buried recently?"

She shook her head. Wonder filled her. Could she be staring at a relic from the 1800s? Could she be standing next to one?

"Inside here is the idiocy of young boys. We have saved, in a snuff box, a lock of hair from all of the sisters in the house, whom we kissed."

"What?"

"Too true. The foibles of youth. We ran these back woods as youths, and well, innocent enough I suppose, but their hair inside will show I know of what I speak."

He knelt on the ground, Jane close beside, and softly peeled back the dirt on the top of the box.

"We could do this in better circumstances, perhaps preserve more of this evidence."

"I am impatient to prove the truth of my words."

She nodded. "Be careful."

He started to lift the lid, its softness falling apart as he tilted it back, away from the contents inside.

The snuff box itself was in better condition, though still appeared to be rotting. He finished opening its lid and then muttered, "Blast that woman."

"What?" Jane scooted closer, trying to see over his arms.

"She's gone and swapped out our things."

Disappointment filled Jane. "That's convenient."

He ignored her, carefully pulling out bits and pieces of what was left in the box. "The bits of parchment are here, though. Look and see."

She peered in, holding her breath so as not to upset the contents.

Then he grunted. "Here it is." He lifted out a ring, covered in dirt. "My old signet."

She gasped. "Are you sure?"

"Of course I'm sure. I must have lost it the one summer we had a kissing contest amongst us." His eyes found hers. "I apologize for my frankness. I told you it wouldn't show my most favorable side."

"I'm still not convinced this is proof."

He rubbed the ring on his shirt. "I'm not looking at it, just cleaning it. Here." He handed it to her without looking. "I'll describe it."

She rubbed it more, trying to get dirt out of the crevices so that the design was recognizable. As he started on one end of the ring and spoke of details all the way to the other end, some of which she had to further clean the ring with spit in order to see, she widened her eyes. "It's really you? My Regency man?"

His eyes clouded. "Pardon me?"

She stammered, "I mean, you really are from 1817?"

"Yes, and as far as I know, I'm still there, having a weird dream."

"No, you're not. You're here in my time. And this is the best news I've ever heard."

She wanted it to be true. So far, all the evidence he provided showed he really at least thought he was from 1817. How could this ring be there? No one had opened that box in decades, if not two hundred years. Pictures of his ring could be in research books somewhere. Easily proven. Everything about him seemed real. Not only was her Regency man clearly and truly standing right in front of her, but he was more handsome in person than she had ever imagined, and he unlocked the key to all her research questions. If only she could convince him to stick around in her century. With any luck, he was trapped here—she cringed as she thought such a selfish thing—at least for now, trapped for a short amount of time, she amended.

## CHAPTER 9

*A*lgernon pushed the muddied ring onto his finger and followed Jane up the lawn toward the great house. Everywhere he looked he saw evidence of time passing. And differences in the gardens. Even in the moonlight the hedges looked different. They had tried to maintain the same foundations, he noticed. And the fountains. He stopped to peer over a hedge. Some of the fountains were the same.

Jane came back to stand beside him. "What?"

"That's original. Much older now, but it's something that's familiar to me." Instead of comforting, though, the obvious wear and weather on the piece depressed him, proving he had well and truly left his time.

She squealed. "You're like a regular verifier of facts. I cannot believe my luck." She picked up her pace.

Algernon tried not to feel overwhelmed. He had trusted her when she was back at the house, but now she seemed like a totally different person, with a purpose far beyond merely helping him.

She picked up her pace, almost running across the lawn.

He cleared his throat and stopped walking. And waited.

At length she turned around to talk to him and came running back. "What's the matter? Don't you want to get inside? There's so much I have to see in there, to verify. I'm certain if we tell them you're a relation, they'll let you see their old artifacts. The letters. Do you know how amazing this is?"

He didn't answer. When did the situation stop being about him and start being about her insatiable desire to research?

She stopped. "Are you okay?"

He groaned. "There's that *okay* word again."

"I'm sorry." She placed a hand on his arm. "I'm being completely selfish here. I shall try to speak in a manner more like that to which you are accustomed."

He slowed his breathing. "A bit better, thank you."

"And I shall endeavor to walk at a civilized pace."

"Yes, that too would be appreciated."

"And perhaps I shall explain a few things?" She put a hand on his arm. "Or even better, perhaps I should listen. How are you handling all of this new information?"

"I'm not doing well, to tell you the truth. There are some real concerns I would like addressed, perhaps this moment if possible."

She held her hands out. "We'll have to delay a bit longer than this moment, but we will attempt to puzzle through."

"For example, what precisely do you hope to accomplish at this home?"

"In my world, I have employment."

"Your family is in trade?"

"Not quite that, but now, all these years later, men and women work, every day, for their income."

"How dreadful. Are there no nobles?"

"There are. We are standing on the property of some of the remaining nobles. And they are an old family, old enough to know who you are."

"Shall we tell them?"

"No, I think it best to move forward as though you are the distant grandson. The resemblance is obvious and will help us."

"And why do we need to wheedle our way in here?"

"Because, for my employment, I study your day, this family in particular, and I would like to know more about their daughters."

He snorted. "Not sure why. They're the biggest blue-stocking opinionated lot of women I've ever known." The irony of his disgruntlement at strong-willed women with opinions needled at him even through all his confusion.

She smirked. "And you kissed them."

He felt his face heat. True enough. He should have never disclosed such a thing. "And you wish to have a look inside, see their bits of things from my day, is that it?"

"Precisely. And if you don't mind, I'd love to spend some time studying you." She raised an eyebrow. "And getting to know you. For educational purposes, of course." She stepped nearer. "Not just educational purposes. I have something I need to tell you, some time."

"I suppose I have all the time in the world. Let's see what this is about, shall we?"

She turned and would have continued at her brisk pace but he called out. "Jane. Won't they all be abed at this hour?"

She sighed. "They will. I've been attempting to mull my way through that problem."

"You think we can just show up at the doorstep, proclaiming my familial connection, and then traipse on in?"

"Yes, I was thinking that. But perhaps we should return tomorrow?"

"And leave a card, yes."

She looked uncomfortable.

"You don't leave cards anymore?"

"No, we don't. Look, when you realize all the wonderful changes to the world, you are never going to want to leave."

The sick feeling in his gut squirmed and rolled. Perhaps. But for some reason, of all the parts of home that would come to him in that moment, his neglect of his father's study, his refusal to care for the estate, the tenants, all came barreling to the forefront of his mind; he regretted leaving things as he had.

She pulled out her magical carriage summoner and tapped into it again like she had earlier. "I'm calling for another carriage. We'll return tomorrow."

They made their way to the road. This time she walked slowly enough that he was able to offer his arm. The simple normalcy of such a gesture comforted him. "Thank you, Jane."

She squeezed his forearm. "For what?"

"For being here with me through this, for believing me. It can't have been a coincidence that it was you who found me."

Her quiet expression did not concern him. Large important things were happening, things that deserved thought.

"I think I've spent my life preparing to meet you." She turned to him. "We must get some sleep, but tomorrow, some-time tomorrow I wish to tell you more about that painting you're in."

Then a bright light shone in their faces. "Hands up."

"How dare you treat me thus, get that light out of my face."

He couldn't see anything, and the light shone a searing path through the front of his head and into his brain.

Jane raised her hands. "We're on his property where we don't belong. You're not a duke here. Put your hands up." Her words were still intelligible though she spoke through gritted teeth.

"But technically I am a duke here as well as there, am I not? Or at least my descendants are. Do you suppose I have descendants?" *My word.* He hadn't even thought of that. Why waste time at this home? He should be traveling back to his own family estate. A ping of regret nudged him at the thought. For then this remarkable journey would be over.

The same man's gruff voice said, "State your business here. You are trespassing on private property."

Jane stepped forward, hands still up. "This is a Ramsbury, related to the Duke of Shelton, and we were here to relive a childhood memory."

"Of my great grandfather." They would have to get their stories straight if they were to continue in this tale.

"Ramsbury? The Duke of Shelton?" The light turned off, and Algernon blinked until he made out the dark figure of a man standing in front of him. "If you'll come with me, please?"

The man turned and walked toward the front door of the house.

Jane reached for Algernon's hand and laced her fingers in his. The shock of her skin against his own filled him with a pleasing sensation up his arm. And at the same time it thrilled him, the feel of skin on skin comforted, and he tightened his hold on her hand.

The man led them through the front door and continued on into the house without comment. He walked up a set of stairs toward the back of the house, and they followed silently.

The house bore little resemblance to the home he had visited so often as a child. The floors were different, walls, furnishings, even the stair rails were redone.

But as they moved farther away from the front part of the home, more signs of the old house caught his eye. The creak of the wood, the uneven flooring, the woodwork on the ceiling all brought memories.

At last the man stopped in front of a door at the end of a long hallway. He took out a ring of keys. "It is a common folklore among the members of the staff that one day a man will show up at our door. He may be alone or he may have a woman with him, and if he calls himself by the name of Ramsbury, Duke of Shelton, we are to let him in. And if he can produce proof by way of a ring . . ." The man waited, eyebrows raised.

Algernon held out his rather filthy hand and even filthier ring.

The man sniffed. "If he can show us the ring, then we are to show him the contents of this room. But, Your Grace, I'm going to have to insist that you, and your guest, wash your hands first and then use the gloves provided while handling the contents of this room."

"Certainly." Algernon moved across the hall to the room indicated. Jane joined him, and they stood at the sink, hands under running water, soaping as best they could to get all the dirt from their fingernails. "The continuing water, just flowing out, is convenient."

Jane smiled. "I've never heard such an understated appreciation for indoor plumbing."

"You make no sense to me, woman."

At last they felt sufficiently clean, and the man unlocked the door.

They entered an old and musty room. Jane touched something on the wall and the room lit, all the corners, every part of the space looked as though it were day. He shook his head. "Remarkable."

"Like I said, stick around. You're not gonna want to leave."

The man closed the door behind him, and they heard it lock.

"Should we be concerned we are locked inside this room and no one else knows where we are?" Algernon made a face.

"Any other room, I'd say yes, but in here, no. This is the quest of my life, right here. I can't wait to see what treasures I can find."

Jane's eyes glistened with happiness and curiosity. And he could relate to that insatiable urge for knowledge. It was the reason he'd traveled all the way to Twickenham in the first place to begin this infernal journey. He watched Jane carefully peel back the lids of boxes. Infernal journey? He had to wonder. Was it perhaps less of hell and more of heaven? He could never regret meeting Jane, and his eyes had been opened to a world of possibility. He definitely wasn't bored. Thinking back to everything Nellie had said, she had promised he would return and no one would know he had been gone. So what did he have to lose? He may as well observe these new ways, enjoy the conveniences of their day, and learn what he could.

Jane's hair fell down around her as she started reading old documents, her face alight with the passion of learning, her skin soft, her hair shining from the light of the room. He knew his heart was well on its way to being caught. And he didn't know if leaving a portion of one's heart in the future was such a wise idea.

*Unless he didn't go back.* That idea might have appealed to him last week, but now he didn't want to desert his responsibilities completely. Putting them off indefinitely had been the simple act of laziness, but deciding to leave his estate forever?

Nellie. She would have answers. He feared in time, he'd be in a most unenviable position of choosing between the lovely Jane and the only life he'd ever known.

# CHAPTER 10

*J*ane and Algernon worked until the sun came up and well past lunch before Jane became aware of her surroundings. So lost in the letters, the documents, the artifacts, she barely noticed Algernon at her side. Their tea, and then their lunch, sat cold in the corner. But her throat itched, and she needed a drink. Her gown hung loosely and slipped off her shoulder for the umpteenth time. She would have impatiently jerked it back up without thinking, but Algernon's warm hand enveloped the soft skin, and she sucked in her breath. He stood close, his eyes earnest, searching her face. Then his voice near her ear, "You are driving me to distraction, all morning, wearing nothing but this slip of a thing. Please. Stop. Eat. And perhaps ask for something daytime appropriate to wear?"

She swallowed, suddenly intensely aware of Algernon. He left his hand on her shoulder but a moment more, and then he let it drop. Her smile felt weak, everything felt weak. She wanted nothing more than to throw herself into his arms.

"Perhaps we could have some of those sandwiches, and a drink of water?"

He nodded. Then he placed his hand at her cheek. "You fascinate me. I've watched you, lost in your learning for hours this morning, and I've never seen the like. Imagine if I'd spent even a small amount of the same on something of import to me."

His praise washed over her like a warm breeze and sent welcome shivers up her back. She stepped nearer, and he seemed as though he might embrace her, but instead he reached for her hand. He peeled back her research gloves. "I do admit to appreciating the fact that you refuse to wear gloves, usually." They walked to the table together.

Jane cradled her newest find in one hand. She wanted to get his opinion on it right away. "I've found something."

"Jane. We must eat before we talk about any more of your finds. You have found many somethings."

They both took a seat at the table. "But this something is a letter to you. Sealed."

"What?" He took it from her outstretched hand. "The Lichfield family seal." He broke it, the wax crumbling with age in his hands. Then he gently opened the paper.

Jane rushed to his side. Her heart stuttered. "How can this be?" Inside the letter was another, closed, sealed, with one word on the front, *Jane.* "Do you know another Jane?"

His eyes were already scanning the page. She leaned across him, pressing against him to see.

He shifted away. "Please, woman. I'm doing my best not to pull your partially clothed self against me and kiss you senseless."

She felt her face burn. "I . . . I'm sorry." Then she tried to see over his shoulder without touching him. "Perhaps if you shared . . ."

"It is my correspondence after all."

"True." She sat beside him for about two breaths, then stood. "Could you at least read it aloud?"

He read in silence a moment more, then handed it to her. He pocketed the other letter.

*Dear Algie,*

*If you are reading this, you have truly made the leap. I wonder what time you have landed. We wanted you to know we are well. When you return you will likely hear of our distancing ourselves from society in our time, but we are having the grandest adventures, as I'm sure you will understand shortly. Never fear. Enjoy your own adventure. It is a gift to you to be treasured long after you return. And if Jane be the one, give this letter to her in the front entryway of your home in London. Perhaps we shall cross paths in our time or another. I suspect we will, else how do I know you will receive this letter at all?*

*Also, happy to return your ring. I'm not sorry I kept it from you. You deserved it, after all, and now look what it's got you.*

*Happy travels,*

*Constance Lichfield*

Jane sat back, stunned. More time travelers? These very women she would study? She didn't know how to explain any of it. Up until this moment she had still doubted. Everything could have been some sort of intricate plan, some deception that even Algernon believed, some invention of his mind. But now, she had nothing but proof. The letter was surely dated to the 1800s. She'd seen him break the seal. Even a cursory glance told her that much.

She had taken picture after picture on her phone and took

another one of this letter. "And the other?" She held out her hand. "Shall we read it?"

He shook his head, eating bites of their lunch. "You saw what it said. We are to give it to someone named Jane, if she be the one, and not until you or she is standing in my London townhome." He took a sip of water. "Which I've been meaning to bring up. I would like to visit my estate, if you will."

A knock at the door had them both standing, and Jane hurriedly tied her robe tighter about her person. She should have asked for clothing, or changed before they left, grabbed boots, or her pelisse. But she didn't know she would be anywhere besides a dark property of someone's manor.

The footman opened a door and a woman, regal in her bearing, wearing a pink skirt suit, hair curled gently around her face, stepped into the room. Her gaze traveled over Jane's attire, resting on her hair in such a quick assessing glance that Jane was left wanting to defend or explain her appearance. But she had no opportunity. The woman stepped into the room, all grace, and held out her hand to Algernon. "Hello, Your Grace, pardon the lack of introductions, but I'll just have to do it myself. I am Lady Anna. And I'm so pleased you have come."

Algernon bowed over her hand. "The pleasure is mine. I must thank you for receiving us at such an odd hour and for accommodating our research."

"I presume you have found everything to your liking?"

"Yes, of course. Most enlightening in many respects." He dipped his head. "And might I introduce Jane Sullivan?"

"Thank you, yes, charmed." She held out a hand for Jane to take.

"Pleased to meet you. Are we in your home?"

"My family's. For many generations." She looked meaning-

94

fully at Algernon. And then turned serious eyes to Jane. "I hope you've found what you're looking for."

"I have. My research will be richly benefitted, my dissertation, a landmark piece on women. I'm most grateful."

"You can thank His Grace. And it is our hope that you put together all your research in a most expeditious manner so that it might be published as soon as possible, while you are yet with us. Shall we sit? I feel some explanations are in order."

Jane's mind spun. What was she talking about, while I am yet with them?

Algernon held out Lady Anna's chair. "Yes, of course." He then held one for Jane. She felt a bit bumbling next to this perfectly poised woman. She would have given anything for her own pantsuit. She tried to pretend she had one on.

Algernon sat, and they both looked expectantly at this new Lady Anna.

"You must know we all view your arrival with the greatest amount of curiosity."

Jane cleared her throat. "The man outside last night said that the staff has talked about Ramsbury specifically for several decades?"

Lady Anna raised her eyebrows, as if surprised Jane spoke. "Did he now? Yes, I imagine that's true." She turned back to Algernon. "Very few know the details of your special circumstances. The staff view this as some sort of legend-come-to-life experience." She talked of the staff as though their thoughts were amusing, insignificant.

Jane didn't even know the details of their special circumstances, but she was all ears to all the thoughts about what could be going on here.

"But those of us who do have decided to move forward with the following depiction of what has happened." She smiled at them, an interesting, public smile. Jane wondered what went on inside her head, how to break that shell. "We have decided that you are a direct descendant of the Ramsbury family. And it was just discovered because of your remarkable resemblance to this painting." She waved her hand, and a staff member who must have been waiting by the door for just such a summons entered with a large canvas, covered in fabric. He placed it on an easel and lifted the fabric.

Jane gasped and held a hand to her mouth. The very painting from her book. Her Regency man.

Lady Anna raised an eyebrow, then turned to Algernon. "An obvious likeness, do you agree?"

He cleared his throat. "To be clear, that is me."

She shifted in her seat. "Yes, and some will hold by that story while others in the family prefer to talk of things instead in the manner in which I'm describing. Shall we continue?"

He nodded.

Jane listened with half an ear. She rose to take a closer look. The artwork was incredibly well preserved. She lifted her phone. "May I take pictures?"

Lady Anna nodded. "We would like to introduce you to society, to announce your existence to the world, so to speak, at a gala this Friday."

Jane moved back to the table and sat again in her chair.

Algernon nodded. "And so I'm to be presented as my own grandson by many generations?"

"Yes, precisely. And might I suggest we attend together? I do believe my own ancestors would be pleased at the thought."

Algernon peered closer. "Are you?" He sat back and smiled. "I see it. You are a Lichfield."

She nodded, a lovely pink lining her cheeks.

Jane gasped. "Then it's true. The sisters did marry."

Lady Anna turned to Jane. "And you may stay as long as you like to complete your research." She turned back to address Algernon, waving her hand over Jane as if she were an object of interest. "I'm happy you have staff to take care of these things for you, Your Grace."

Algernon's face clouded with confusion. "Is she not . . ."

"A noble? Heavens no. Jane, you are American, if I'm not mistaken."

She nodded. "Yes, of course." She turned to Algernon. "You knew that."

He shook his head. "Yes, of course. I wasn't viewing it in the same manner in which I am now. So England has its peerage still. The families are all here."

She nodded. "Yes, though I, for one, am happy for the addition of another younger duke." Her eyes widened, and she smiled, a slow, willing smile.

Jane wanted to gag and throw water in Lady Anna's face all at the same time. But Algernon seemed taken with her, or at least seemed to think he'd found his people.

"What about our enactment?" Jane had already planned to stop attending, had planned to hole up in here with Algernon while she read and researched. She imagined he had cared little for it either. Perhaps it would be good for him to meet his people, spend some time, perhaps even see his family. But she hated the thought of sending him off with Lady Anna.

"I don't much care for those people. Do you?" Algernon still relied on her. She was warmed by the thought.

"No, let's send word we will not be returning. Perhaps there is someone who could send over our things?"

Algernon rested a hand on top of hers. "And you'll be coming to the gala too, will you not?"

"Well, I . . ."

"Surely not." Lady Anna's condescension dripped off her fingers as she waved them about. "We are not her, how do you say . . . set? She would feel uncomfortable, out of her element."

Jane bristled.

Algernon's soft pressure on her fingers calmed a tempest that was rising. His eyes smiled, and he turned to Lady Anna and said, "I would very much like to attend your gala with Jane at my side."

Her eyes narrowed for the briefest second and then widened. "Of course. It will be arranged. We will send a car at five on Friday. And we will take care of your things at the enactment and your withdrawal from the event."

Even though she found it difficult to stomach the blatant snobbery, Jane couldn't believe her luck. "Thank you, Lady Anna. This is all very accommodating of you. I admit I still don't know what's going on, but I have an earnest desire to become involved, to learn all that I can."

Lady Anna briefly acknowledged that Jane had spoken and then turned to Algernon. "And perhaps, Your Grace"—she raised an eyebrow—"it is time to have a bit of fun besides?" She slid a card across the table to him. "A group of us get together now and again, on yachts from one of our villas, rotating the location. I think you would find it vastly entertaining." She stood when he took the card.

He turned to Jane. "You said you don't do calling cards anymore."

"She won't understand everything about our set. It's just as before, where you're from. She's a commoner."

Jane injected, "And yet, we do have business and personal cards we hand out. Lady Anna is correct. Our world is very different now than it used to be. In many ways I prefer the older ways of doing things. I appreciate the nobility, their manners and charms, but one thing has drastically changed, and that is the fact that they don't control the world any more. They are more a small cliquish group clinging to each other for notoriety and popularity. While the rest of the world actually gets something done."

Lady Anna stood. "Spoken like a true commoner. You will find differing opinions wherever you go, I'm afraid. I look forward to seeing you Friday." She turned to Jane. "Good luck on your research. We do wish you the best of luck and find your studies fascinating. Especially the women among us would most ardently like you to succeed in your efforts."

*Interesting.* "Thank you." She stopped a curtsy that was in the making in her mind and walked back to the boxes and paperwork so that she could continue where she left off.

Algernon and Lady Anna chatted in the doorway. She was close and too cozy for Jane's liking. No one had dibs on her Regency man yet, not until Jane could figure out who he was supposed to be in her life, and not until they'd had a chance to be together themselves. Was that selfish? She thought not. But what chance did she stand against the likes of Lady Anna and her wealth and title? Jane knew the Regency rules. In Algernon's day, she would never have caught his eye. And . . . she needed to think sensibly. He would likely be going back to his time. And what good would it do her to fall for some guy she would pine after for the rest of her life and never see again?

Oh the irony. She'd already spent enough time dreaming of her Regency man. She wandered back over to the painting and studied his face, his grin so full of knowing. What did he know? What caused that smile? One thing she knew she must do, and that was ask him every single question she had ever had about the Regency era.

# CHAPTER 11

*A*lgernon brought in a stack of the dailies, Lady Anna had called them. She wasn't staying at the house, but she had stopped by at least once a day the last couple days. Clothes had arrived for him, newly purchased, and he had taken to wearing them instead of his typical attire from home. Jane continued to wear Regency dresses. She claimed she liked them better. He liked her in them. It brought a sense of stability to his emotions.

Jane sat at a desk she had moved over by the windows and studied another set of documents. Her hair fell down around her shoulders, and with the light shining just so on her features, he could have been staring at an angel. She represented so much that he loved in women back home plus none of the things that bothered him. She didn't appear to be all that enamored with him, as far as he could tell, or rather, she was interested, obviously affected by his touch, but not so deferential as to lose her personality. She allowed her hair to be worn down, and she did not use gloves. Plus she spoke her mind. She studied more than most men of his acquaintance and was not only unashamed, but quite proud of her education.

She looked up and sat back with her mouth open. "Wow! You look incredible!"

He laughed. "Do you think so?" He had chosen to wear one of his suits. The other more casual attire just felt wrong.

"Lady Anna knows how to shop. I'll give her that."

"'I'll give her that'? What does this mean?" He had asked her to start speaking more in modern language so that he could become accustomed.

"It's like, I concede she has that good quality about her."

"Ah. You don't like her."

Jane huffed. "I like her fine. She just puts on airs."

"But she's a noble. That's how we are, are we not?"

"I know. And when I think of you in your time, it doesn't bother me half as much." A soft circle of pink colored her cheeks. "I confess I always imagined myself to be a noble like the rest of you."

"And she never neglects to remind you of your place."

"Precisely. And it rankles even more because only here in her house or with her people does her status matter."

Algernon reached for her hand. "It doesn't matter to me where you're concerned."

"I wonder if it would matter if you were home, what you would think if you met me there."

An uncomfortable pinch twinged his heart. "I guess that would depend under what circumstances we met. I am ashamed to say, I don't much admire the person I was only two hundred years and ten days ago."

She laughed, as he knew she would. "I'm getting used to the idea. You're really from a time two hundred years past."

He pulled her close. "Might we leave the house, tour, do

something? I have no idea what my modern-day Britain looks like."

"We will. I'm almost finished. This you see here is the last of it."

He shook his head. "You're remarkable."

"The next part will be the most enjoyable . . . for me."

"Oh, and what is that?"

"Where I ask you about two hundred million questions about all this. You're mentioned more than once, you know."

He smiled. "I'm not surprised. We visited here as children and as youth often."

"And what of your possible marriage to them?"

He sucked in a breath and then coughed. "I don't know. It was never mentioned to me. If the women in the family wished such a thing, my father never joined them in supporting it, or opposing."

"There was talk in one correspondence, where perhaps your father may have reached out to their father for the hand of one. I think there might have been some financial trouble mentioned?"

The twinge in Algernon's heart sharpened and hurt. "I am ashamed to say I suspect there to be much wrong on the estate, but since my father's death I have been unable to face the prospect of having to solve all the problems he may have caused and spent much of my time behaving as though my ignoring the trouble would make it go away. Like I said, uncouth." He cringed when the word left his lips. And he noticed that pinched lips were the natural shape of lips when saying the word *uncouth*. Such a realization explained so much of the matrons' response to him.

"Let's look up your estate, your home!"

"Lady Anna already has. She showed me yesterday the place

has been sold and is now a library and museum. We can tour it. She offered to take me, but I had hoped you would come."

Jane looked at the last of her work, then at him, and stood. "Let's go. I can finish this tonight, and then we have the gala tomorrow."

"She sent clothes for you as well. She said you cannot go in period costume. Though I'm sure I have no idea what she's talking about. You look perfectly timeless to me."

Jane rewarded him with a grin and came toward him, hands out. "Thank you for everything, Algernon. Because of you and all of this, I will make huge strides in my research. My paper is certain to be accepted with all these original ideas and just might alter the way we understand the past." She reached for the magazines in his hands. "What is all this?"

"The press releases for my return. Lady Anna and her press team have been drafting the words they will use to describe me. They had a photographer here the other day for pictures."

"Algernon! Holy cow, you look totally hot!"

"Pardon me?"

She laughed. "That's what a girl says about a guy who would attract any girl." She reached up and brushed off his shoulder. "But it's not a particularly genteel manner of speaking."

He pulled her into his arms. "But you meant it?" He loved the way she willingly molded to him, her soft frame like heaven in his hands.

She nodded. The slight pink to her cheeks was endearing.

"Attract most girls? Or just one? You?"

She rested her hands on his arms, pressed against his chest. Her eyes widened, and she looked up into his in such an open way, he wanted to take her away forever to be his. "You look amazing. I thought you looked good in breeches, but you pull off Armani better than anyone I've ever seen."

Pleased, he looked down at his suit coat. "Is this Armani?"

"It is, it's the name of the tailor. The designer."

"I like Armani."

"Yeah, most people do. It's more of a casual suit, though, for people of your stature. It's like the everyday Armani wear. There are other designers who make custom clothing just for you."

"Ah, like my personal tailor, the modistes for the women, in London."

"Yes, exactly. Your suit for the gala is like that."

"And your dress as well?"

"I'm not sure, but it's lovely. I'm very happy with it."

The butler knocked on their door. "You have a visitor."

Algernon reluctantly let her leave his arms, and he led her out of their study room. They locked the door behind them and then descended the stairs together.

Charles Smithy stood near the front door, a mocking raised eyebrow eyeing their descent. "Now, don't you make quite a pair? The eternal Regency woman and the newly found duke."

"Hello Charles." Jane walked toward him and kissed his cheek. "How are you? How's the enactment?"

He waved his hand. "Now that you're gone, the fun has fizzled into nothing but mindless dribble. They've even delayed the contest announcement until the very end."

"Oh, I do hope you win."

Algernon came to stand at her side, hoping she wouldn't reveal more.

"I would have been a shoe-in had you not deserted the group. Tell me, have they let you take a look? Is it as useful as they say?"

Algernon motioned they should walk to the door. "I've glanced in the room. It's for family and friends only. Looks like a dark room full of boxes to me." The butler opened the door for them, and a car pulled forward. "We're going to tour my old family estate. Perhaps we could get together before you all leave, a game of whist or some other such thing?"

Charles's eyes narrowed, but he kept up his charm for Jane's sake, Algernon assumed. He, of course, recognized the man's subtle duplicity as that of all men trying to impress a woman, but he didn't trust him otherwise either. "Let's make it happen, or drinks at a local bar. I find the enactment growing tedious."

Jane gasped.

"I know." Charles shook his head. "You could keep it up for months on end, but I'm nearing the end of my tolerance." He nodded his head. "I hope you enjoy a reacquaintance with your heritage, Your Grace."

Charles stepped into his own limo. Algernon and Jane stepped into the one behind. Algernon leaned back in his seat. "I could get used to this, much preferred to the carriages of my day."

Jane's face grew troubled. "Not all cars are quite this nice. Mine is much less comfortable."

He reached for her hand. "Jane. Whatever your status, your income here, it has no bearing on the remarkable woman I am coming to know."

She nodded and looked out the window. "I wonder what we'll find in your home."

They rode in silence for a moment. Jane adjusted her dress five times before Algernon finally said, "You are starting to make me nervous with your fidgeting. What is it?"

Her lip turned up in half a smile. "I have an idea that I want to suggest, but I'm unsure how you will respond."

He picked up her hand. "I will respond in the best way I know how."

"You are so sincere."

"You are my lifeline here. I think you would be anywhere."

"We haven't talked about you returning home, or if you want to or how. But I was wondering, hoping, that you could delay that a little while?"

His hand tightened around her own. "It is a topic I'm loath to address at the same time I am anxious to. I left things in a terrible state. I know not how terrible, but I do have to return."

She nodded. "But perhaps you could linger here for a time?" Her eyes, vulnerable, asking, were too much for him. He would grant even the smallest of her desires were he able, and this, seeming to be of such importance to her, he was prepared to do whatever she asked.

"Come to America with me."

He faltered. "What?"

"It's not like it used to be, in your time. We get there in one day. I have to return to work next week, and I can't leave you here, and I can't stay. And I could really use your help with my research, and . . ." Her eyes found his. "I don't want to lose you yet."

His heart sped up at her admission. "I never want to leave your side. I wish I could promise our parting was not to be expected. And as usual, there is much you just said I don't understand. Like how you arrive in America in one day, but let's start with the most important. Where you go, I go. If we must return for your responsibilities in America, then we do so. Let us accomplish all we must here in England before we go. Much will depend on what we find in my home."

She breathed out in so much relief, he scooted closer and pulled her into his arms. "You never have to worry about my loyalties. I feel we have been placed together by Fate herself."

Her arms, squeezed around him, made him feel strong. A strong desire to lift her, to place her on his shoulders and turn in circles so that all might see her, filled him. At the same time, he wanted to be strong, a protection to her. "Let's make your paper the best anyone has ever read."

"Thank you, Algernon. This means everything to me."

They slowed and pulled into the entrance to Algernon's London townhome. "Shelton Public Historical Library."

"I almost can't bear the sight of my home turned into a public museum." He ran a hand through his hair. "Had I only taken a moment to preserve the estate, something, anything." The pain in his heart felt sharp, cutting into his breathing. "Let's be about it then; nothing to be gained in the delay."

# CHAPTER 12

"*I* love that they made your home a library, if it couldn't be a home. Have you read anything more about your family? What happened to them?"

"Lady Anna said they are unsure where the nearest descendant is. When the estate fell apart so long ago, the family fell into poverty, spread out, and their identity became lost over the centuries. She said my family is covered in some school courses as an example of the dying nobility in England."

The driver opened their door, and they slid out. Her cell phone dinged. She hadn't been keeping in touch with Chelsea, or anyone at home. *Call when you get a minute. Very important.*

She wouldn't request it if it wasn't truly vital. "Algernon, I need to make a phone call. You go on ahead."

Chelsea picked it up on the first ring. "Jane, we need you to be amazing. They're cutting funding to the society."

Her feet stopped moving forward. She couldn't think straight. "But why?"

"Yes, unless we can prove we provide some unique inclusion to the Jane Austen conversation, we are out of funding.

And even if we do contribute, now we know how precarious our situation is. We need money and unique research now."

"I've got the research. Don't you worry. Enough to knock even your socks off."

"Glad to hear it."

Jane's mind started to spin. "And I might have some ideas on how to raise some money while we're at it."

"Well, whatever you do, do it fast and then come back. This stress alone is killing me."

"I'll be there as soon as I can. But what I'm doing over here is precisely what might save us."

"I know. Glad we sent you. Keep me posted. An email, an outline, some shred of hope."

"Will do. And don't worry. It's gonna work out." Jane hoped so. She knew her research would not disappoint. How could it with so many original sources, including a walking, breathing man? But they needed funds. Lots of funds.

She put her phone back in her reticule. She had to admit, walking around in Regency attire outside of a typical manor house was more inconvenient than lovely. No pockets, at least not convenient ones. The fabric was thin, and she hadn't brought a pelisse or anything with her.

Frustrated she had missed some of Algernon's first sights of his old home, she hurried to find him. The front door creaked open at her touch. She entered just what she expected to find: a small entryway where a butler might take their things. Then a hallway to her front, rooms off to her side. She knew they would connect, one room with the next, all through this level of the home.

She made her way to the front parlor. The room was now cordoned off as a museum, displaying period pieces. Normally she would study each one, testing herself to see which were truly period pieces and which duplicated and added to the collection to help round out the room, but today she was anxious to find Algernon.

As she moved to the next space, the noise of a large group of people reached her and she hurried toward it.

"It's uncanny. Look at the likeness."

"Did I not tell you? See, turn to the side, just like the portrait."

Gasps resounded.

Jane smiled, and she wondered what Algernon thought of all the new attention.

He posed in front of his own portrait up on the wall. When she entered, his eyes lit and he grinned, one hand still in a pocket, sitting as though someone were still taking his portrait.

The ladies turned and eyed her with no small amount of curiosity.

She stepped closer. "Hello. Have you found his portrait then?"

He winked and then turned to face it. "We have. Just as everyone tells me. We could easily be brothers were he alive today."

"Brothers! No, twins." One of the ladies with a nametag pointed up to the image. "If I didn't know it to be impossible, I'd say you and he were one and the same. I'd know, wouldn't I? Staring at it all hours of the day and night."

Algernon raised his eyebrows. "Well, I do hope his mug didn't grow too tiresome, such as it is."

"No, not at all. I don't suppose I shall ever tire of him . . . or it." She reached up as if to touch it, then lowered her hand. Her cheeks colored, and Algernon edged away.

Jane laughed and asked one of the ladies, "Shall we continue our tour? Might I ask how many of the exhibits are all original pieces from the home?"

"I will tell you that as we go from room to room, don't you worry," the guide stated.

Algernon moved to stand beside Jane. "And the family? I'd love to hear what happened to them."

"I'm sure you would. How's that got to feel? To go to bed one night a nobody and then waking up the next morning a blooming duke." She stopped and put a hand on her mouth. "Beggin' your pardon, Your Grace." Then she giggled. "You used to that yet? Everyone your gracin' you all the time?"

"I shall try to grow accustomed." He was obviously not amused.

Jane rested a hand on his arm.

He tipped a head closer to her, and she thrilled at his nearness. "Everything well with your phone call?" His eyes held concern. Perhaps her worry was more visible than she would have liked.

"Some concerns at work, with my employment. I do need to get back."

He rested a hand over hers, and she felt grateful for this longtime custom. "Then we'd best be about it. The gala's tomorrow. Perhaps we could leave Saturday morning."

She nodded; perhaps at the gala she could find more sources of funds and some help with her idea. She cleared her throat. "How would you like to help me earn some more money for our historical society? It involves breeches and a horde of women anxious to spend time with you."

He raised an eyebrow. "I'm intrigued."

They entered the last room of the tour, the study. Algernon paused in the doorway. "Everything in the room is the same. The shelves, the wood paneling, though old and faded, and the desk." He stepped forward to the edge of the cordoned off section. "And there it is."

"Is that your desk?"

His body had tensed, his hands clenched, and then they relaxed and his shoulders drooped. "My father's, really. Newly mine."

The woman leading the tour watched with a confused expression. "This desk dates back to the early nineteenth century. It's one of the original pieces in our set. If I can turn your attention to this exhibit here, we have what experts are guessing is the cause of the fall of the estate. You'll notice on the wall, debts accrued by the late Duke of Shelton. They might seem large, and they were, but not too much to overcome, had the son been attentive. But it appears the young Algernon Ramsbury spent his youth in idleness. He was known for raucous races through Hyde Park, his own bets on horses—"

Algernon snorted. "Never."

She continued as if she hadn't heard. "And practical jokes among the peers. If you read the bottom there, one of the matrons of the time said, "Algernon Ramsbury can often be found laughing in the back of the room, raising havoc wherever he goes and otherwise behaving in an entirely uncouth manner." Algernon cringed beside Jane. She patted his forearm, not sure what to say to a man who was remembered so negatively for over two hundred years.

"We will make this right." He stood taller.

"Yes, I will help you. Perhaps when you're finished, history will change and I will learn of your ancient family line. I will be able to come tour an estate still in the Ramsbury family, with Ramsburys inside, but open to the public on Wednesdays." The thought made her insides hurt. She wasn't ready to give him up. But she hoped to bring a lift back to his shoulders and a hopeful light to his eye.

Their ride back to the Lichfield Estate was quiet. Algernon kept gritting his teeth. She didn't think he was even aware, but his jaw clenched and unclenched and the tension around his eyes started to give her a headache. "Algernon."

He turned to her. "Hmm?"

"I hate to see you like this."

"Something must be done, but I don't see how as I'm two hundred years away." He looked out the window.

"I'm sorry."

He nodded but did not turn back to her.

"Have you considered something perhaps a bit obvious?"

His raised eyebrow did not appear amused.

"No, really, consider this. You have time on your side. That lady, Nellie, said when you returned it would be as if you had never left? Isn't that right?"

He nodded.

"Then you've got nothing to worry about. All this stress is for nothing. You go back, head straight for your study, call for your steward, and then begin."

"Yes, quite right." He turned back to the window.

"Oh come now, Your Grace. In the meantime, let's live it up a little. You're here, in the future. You haven't even had a really good chocolate yet."

His narrowing of the eyes surprised her. "Forgive me if I can't just leap back into congeniality. I've had a rather large blow, learning I was singularly responsible for the collapse of my family's ancient estate and that I am known for its cause a full two centuries later."

She swallowed. "I see, yes. Take as long as you need." She felt terrible. Her own selfish efforts had consumed her, still did. So much so, she hadn't given much thought to Algernon or how he might be affected by all of this.

He returned to staring out the window, and Jane didn't know what else to say to him. She had nothing to compare his experience to in her own life. She owned no property, rented an apartment in New York, and had little connection with her family, ancient or modern.

When they arrived back at the house, they each separated. He to his room and she back to the research room. After reading the last few remaining documents, she wanted to double check facts and make another digital copy of one set of letters, and then she would be finished. A pang of guilt nagged at her. She had been so consumed by this new fascinating research she had ignored his feelings, held off comforting him, or really doing anything at all that wasn't directly related to this project. If she really cared about him, it was time to show it and help.

She opened the door, bent on heading to his room when the loud, high-pitched laughter of Lady Anna carried over to her. "She did not! Oh, Algernon. It's so typical of a commoner. Please, spend some time with our group. You will be so relieved there is yet nobility in England."

"That might be just the thing, Lady Anna. I've mingled with the commoners long enough today."

# CHAPTER 13

*A*lgernon joined Lady Anna in her limo, grateful for her attentiveness. She understood his agony. Algernon needed to associate with other estate owners, with other people of title. They alone would feel the sorrow of having lost something so enormous. He felt as though he'd lost himself. For what was he if not a Ramsbury, a duke, tied to the Shelton estate? With no estate, he was but a man, a shell of a title, with nothing to recommend him. And Jane, as lovely as she was, could not possibly understand his pain. Nor did she even try. She was so caught up in her research she hadn't thought much of anything else.

Lady Anna moved as close as possible to him and placed a hand near his knee. "Thank you for coming. I can't wait to introduce you to everyone. A couple of our group are traveling, but I expect to see Henry, he's the Earl of Henningway. And we have a few barons. The prince might come, the younger one. He's intrigued by your story."

Algernon wondered what story she'd told these people.

"They know only what the press knows."

He nodded. "And it would be wise if we didn't tell them any different?"

"Exactly. Only those associated with Nellie or Twickenham or my own family would be able to understand your unique circumstances."

Lady Anna wore little to no clothing as far as Algernon was concerned. Jane had stuck to Regency attire. She said it was for her own comfort, but he knew she did it to help him. He tried to ignore Lady Anna's long legs that tucked beneath her, her bare ankles, her lovely feet with nothing but some leather strap wrapped about them. She leaned into him. "What's it like, to travel through time?"

He leaned back in his seat farther with the pretense of stretching his back, but he really hoped to dislodge her body from his arm. "It was rather painful, to be honest."

A cloud crossed over her eyes. "Oh."

He chuckled. "But it's been fascinating, completely diverting, and life changing to spend time here, in your day." He didn't want to hurt her feelings. She'd been only lovely to him since he arrived, offering use of her home and transport for him and Jane.

He reached for her hand. "Thank you, Lady Anna, for making this much easier on a sorry duke without land or an estate."

She ran a finger down his thumb. "I can only imagine how shocking all this must be. The others will sympathize. We're all rather excited. It's not often we have a duke among us, unless the prince comes. And Your Grace, you are a duke, land or not. Your title is older than the land around us. You were born a noble and will remain so no matter what time you live in."

The comfort of her words flowed through him, reaching tiny holes of insecurity, binding them up, strengthening him.

"And if I'm not mistaken, can't a duke do whatever he pleases?" A light of adventure lit her face, and he couldn't help grinning in response.

"Just so. Tell me, dear Lady Anna, if you were a duke lost in time without an estate to your name, what would you do?"

She reached over and ran a finger along the back of his neck. "I'd relax. You are desperate for some relaxation." She loosened the tie about his neck, just enough. "And have some fun. Nobles aren't dead, Your Grace. You're about to meet some of the most powerful people in Britain. Let's have a bit of fun tonight, shall we?"

A reckless energy filled him, like he hadn't felt since he left his time. He imagined what he would do were his friends Roderick and Jameson with him. "Let's proceed just as you suggest, then. Fun, reckless abandon, cavorting with the local nobles. How would I say this in modern day language?"

She twisted on their bench and draped her upper body across his. Her lips, a breath away from his own, her eyes sparkling into his, her voice lowered, sultry and sensuous, "A simple 'you're on' would do just fine."

His eyes searched her flawless face, filled with enhancements, powders or other such things. Her full lips waited for his. With the tiniest movement, he could capture them with his own, pull her fully onto his lap. Instead he whispered, "You're on."

They turned onto a busy London street. Nothing about it seemed familiar at all to Algernon.

"Here we are at St. James Street."

"What? This can't be St. James." But the street sign. The corner of St. James and Bond Street. "Are we at White's?" He peered out through the window onto the well-lit street. And yes, they were up the street from White's. It looked the same, but different. "It's unmarked. Is that still White's?"

A soft sigh escaped Lady Anna, and he turned to her.

"It's White's. It's still in use today. The guys are in there right now, but we are meeting down here, at this club."

She was highly bothered. He could tell that much.

"I'm sorry. I cannot abide misogynistic prigs who would associate with anyone in that club."

Algernon didn't understand half of what she said but picked up on her tone. "You are bothered at the men-only aspect."

"Yes, Your Grace. We are not in 1817 any longer." She stopped. "Though I realize that means nothing to you. But now, two hundred years later, we are working against such separatist habits as clubs that exclude one whole gender."

He didn't try to understand but found it interesting. What could a woman possibly want to do in a place like White's? Had women taken to papers and brandy and bets and gambling as well? Women had much more influence in different ways here in 2019, but he hoped they weren't as crass as the men. "What do you see of value in a place like White's? I don't know what it is like today, but there wasn't much there of interest to women." Likely because no women entered. If they had, he was certain the place would have had an altogether different feel, one he would not welcome, were he to be honest. Who wanted colored walls and draperies with frills?

"It's not so much that I desire what might await inside. It's that such a place exists with incredibly archaic membership requirements." She signaled for the driver to open their door. "No matter. I apologize for my—what would you call it? —woolgathering."

"Not quite woolgathering. You were out to fight a battle

and win, but no apology necessary. I'm growing accustomed to the new way of women and their outspoken natures. I find it refreshing and enlightening."

"Coming from an 1817 man. The irony would make me laugh if it wasn't just sad that you, of all people, would appreciate an outspoken and strong woman."

"Oh, I knew a few in my time. They just never let their natures be known on the dance floor. Your ancestors, the sisters, were some of the most outspoken women I know, but at Almack's, when I saw them, they kept their conversation to the weather and the ton gossip." He shook his head. "Such a shame."

Her eyes sharpened. "I suppose they had their reasons, Algie."

She stepped out of the car, leaving Algernon reeling. For a moment, she had sounded just like Anna Lichfield from his time period.

But the moment was gone and she was back to draping across him and smiling for flashes of light. He had learned the flashes were people, taking his likeness. Such an incredible boon to not have to sit for hours on end for one's portrait to be taken.

They pushed their way through a crowd. When Lady Anna nodded to the guards at the door, they let them in immediately.

The club's music played lightly in the background. It sounded instrumental and pleasing. People lingered about in the front foyer area, and Lady Anna led him to a small group on their right.

Others took note of them. Everywhere Algernon looked, eyes were following, but they kept their distance. At last, some semblance of understanding about the importance of waiting to be introduced. People did adhere to the manners of his time at least somewhat.

Lady Anna squeezed his forearm, then she said, "Your Grace Algernon Ramsbury, Duke of Shelton, might I present Lord Tindly, Lord Boxby, and Lord Smithing." They all bowed in turn. Lord Tindly and Lord Boxby looked pleasant enough, but Lord Smithing looked as though he might have punched Algernon if he could. Lord Smithing's eyes slid from him to Lady Anna and back. *Ah, interesting.* Algernon shouldn't, he knew, but he considered having a bit of fun at the baron's expense. He was but a baron, after all.

He smirked, thinking of what Roderick would have done to the poor chap who considered claiming some sort of propri-etary hold over the woman. "Pleased to make your acquain-tance. I find myself in great need of your company, of anyone who could sympathize with my plight."

Lord Boxby lifted his glass. "Would you listen to him? Already sounding just like our stuffed professors at Oxford."

Lord Smithing grunted. "Not much of a plight, waking up one morning to find you're not a commoner, but a noble? Doesn't sound too shabby to me."

Lady Anna lifted her chin. "I think you will find him to be far more enlightening than those celebrated professors and plenty more genteel than the lot of them combined. Some men are born gentlemen whether they know it or not."

"Found a new interest in the genteel and the proper, have you, Anna?" Lord Smithing's eyes searched her own.

"A passing fancy, passing through just like our new duke. Come, let's find a table. Have none of you brought dates?"

Lord Tindly shrugged. But Lord Boxby laughed. "I'm sure one will present herself."

Lady Anna shook her head.

Algernon found them incredibly arrogant. But he supposed himself to be much the same, but never quite so brazen about his conceit in front of the ladies. Or perhaps he was, in his own way. Spending time with Jane had altered his view of the world just enough to leave him questioning how he behaved before.

They were shown their table and, as predicted, were soon joined by three other ladies, as scantily clad as the rest of the women in the room.

Once further introductions were made, he lifted a glass of what they promised was a good brandy. "Let's drink to freedom."

"To freedom."

Everyone downed their drink. He had because he welcomed its numbing effect. But the others gulped the contents of their glasses as though merely water. Shocked the women would follow suit, he watched as they seemed only mildly affected by the drink so far. Lord Boxby ordered another round.

A back door opened and a pounding, almost hypnotic sound came from farther in until the door shut again.

Lady Anna nodded toward the door. "Dance club."

"Do you dance here as well?"

"This club has everything. Let's finish our drinks and we can give it a shot. What say you, ladies?" Lord Boxby seemed to be the fun of the group.

The new women giggled and nodded and would have swooned, Algernon was sure of it, were they able.

Lord Smithing kept up a continued glare in Algernon's direction, interrupted only by his half-hearted effort to entertain the woman at his side.

Algernon started to feel lightheaded after his second drink, but everyone went another round, so he followed suit. Soon he could hardly remember what would ever hold him back from doing anything. He stood. "I wish to see your dances."

Lady Anna whooped. "This will be worth watching, His Grace and the dances of 2019."

They all stood and followed Algernon to the back door.

When it opened, Algernon stopped in his tracks. Smoke swirled, flashing lights hit his face as they moved through the room, and the music pounded in his chest. But he couldn't believe what we was seeing out on the floor.

Lady Anna shouted in his ear, over the music. "A far cry from the waltz." Her face was filled with amusement. The others watched him in confusion. He looked from them to Lady Anna to the dance floor and couldn't think of a single reason not to thoroughly enjoy tonight.

He rushed to the center of the crowd. Everywhere he looked, men and women were engaged in behavior he assumed one would only find in a brothel. Suddenly unsure how to join them, he paused, but Lady Anna stepped into his arms and started bouncing and moving in place, waving her arms, and so he followed suit.

"Dancing like this might be much more palatable at first." She grinned and raised an eyebrow.

"At first! Do you engage in such . . ." He wasn't sure what to call the actions all around him. "Behavior?"

"At times. It can be quite invigorating." She stepped nearer, and his breathing picked up. He imagined it would. Be invigorating.

A waitress brought around more drinks and he downed his next.

"Come on, Algie, this is fun. Let loose and remember, we're here to relax." She started jumping in the air to the faster rhythm. As the drink kicked in, he let go and followed her lead.

Five songs later and with Lady Anna and two other ladies all over him, the music slowed, and he pulled Lady Anna into his arms. "I think I prefer this dancing to the waltz."

"Do you?" She smiled and ran circles on his shoulders with her finger. "Do you remember our first waltz?"

His mind tried to clear. He blinked twice. "Bethany, is it you?"

"No, Algie, but we've danced before, the waltz, right after you'd finished a quadrille with Constance, at the estate."

None of this made sense, and he couldn't make his brain focus.

"I've missed you. We can have anything we want here. Stay. With me." She pressed her body to his, reached a hand around the back of his neck and found his lips with her own.

Fire shot through him at her touch, at their hours of close dancing, at the feel of so much skin beneath his fingers. The fire felt wrong, but he couldn't summon the energy to resist something so pleasurable.

Until a hand grabbed at his shoulder and ripped him away. "That's enough, dukey. Find your own woman." Lord Smithing's knuckles hit his eye before Algernon had a chance to dodge. Vaguely he heard Lady Anna's shouts, but anger boiled up inside. Lord Smithing needed a few rounds at Jacksons to cool off. He'd have to teach him his lesson right here.

He swung and connected with the man's jaw. Lord Smithing stumbled and then ran at him. They swung fists and exchanged blows until the lights went on and men in blue uniforms showed up.

# CHAPTER 14

*A* commoner. So he did see Jane as a commoner. And he'd wanted to get away. Go out, without her. And he was still out, the next morning. Jane shook up the orange juice extra hard. She tried not to think about Lady Anna. She tried to focus again on the few remaining letters she had to read and document. But his hurtful words distracted her. And the truth that no one liked to admit sunk in. Regency-era England was much more than the tiny percentage of people who lived the wealthy lives of nobility. The many thousands more who had no influence on society, no freedom in the country, no recourse if they were wronged, the commoners, those people made up most of England at the time, and they were largely ignored by research. Hers included. A tiny sliver of guilt nagged at her. And as much as she'd loved to pretend, no, *to believe*, that she was in fact a lady in that era and not a forgotten poor woman, as much as she hoped such a thing could be true, she had not a noble drop in her, no name, no title, no land. Then or now. And Algernon was one of the tiny percentage who actually held a noble title now, and in his day, and only associated with others like him. If he had been born in her time, he'd have a royal wedding everyone watched on television.

She shook her head. Dating someone like Algernon would be like calling up one of the thirty single, young male billionaires in the world today, expecting to get a shot. No, it would be like calling up Prince William.

At least she had him for a time for research purposes. And if she were being honest, to spend time with, look at. He was the best-looking man she'd ever met, and hadn't she been staring at his picture for years now? She groaned in frustration. They had both assumed some intricate work of fate brought them here, but perhaps it was not the good kind of fate. Perhaps it was the work of that kind of fate that was twisted and wrong and brought lovers together for a few moments only to then strip them of all hope and doom them to lives of despair. Greek tragedies were full of similar tales.

She snorted. The love tragedies would only apply to the two of them if Algernon shared her same feelings. He seemed perfectly content to go out and enjoy the company of others, others of his class. And so theirs was more a story of unrequited love, a tale as old as the earth itself. But knowing others were doomed just as she was didn't make her feel any better.

Her mind kept circling around him, and she couldn't stand the torture one more minute. She locked the research room, went to her bedroom, changed out of Regency attire to wear her favorite form-fitting jeans and snug sweater. Pleased she would have appalled any and all Regency men and women with her attire, she descended the stairs. A walk on the grounds would help clear her head. She had to make plans, work to save her research team, and write a dissertation. She couldn't be pining for the most fascinating man she had ever or would ever hope to meet.

She rounded the bottom of the huge entry stairway as the butler let in Nellie from Twickenham. Jane stopped. Ever since she had discovered Nellie had some kind of power to make people travel through time, she'd been wary of ever seeing her again. She cleared her throat. "Nellie. Hello."

"Oh good, just the person I need to see. Come, let's sit and talk for a moment." She turned and headed toward the front sitting room.

"Please sit down." Jane indicated a seating of chairs just inside the door.

"I know you are bound to be traveling soon, and I just wanted to give you this." She held out an envelope.

"What's this?"

"Everything Algernon needs in order to return to his time."

"Oh? So he can go, anytime?" A feeling of dread rose in her chest.

"Every full moon. It's detailed precisely in the paperwork." Nellie stood. "I best be off. See that he gets that."

"I will, thank you." Jane's answer sounded weak to her own ears. And she knew her words to be half-baked, and an accurate portrayal of the resolve in her heart. There would be a full moon in two weeks. She was so ashamed to acknowledge that her first reaction was to tear the contents of his instructions to pieces without reading them first. The envelope felt heavy in her hands. But of course she would give it to him. She had to let him know he could go home . . . just as soon as they finished her research. She cringed. Was she contemplating such a thing? No. She would tell him straightaway. She placed the envelope in her bag, ashamed for her moment of selfish temptation.

While her bag was open, the area inside lit with a silent phone notification. It was a phone call from a number she didn't recognize, but it was a local number. She picked it up. "Hello?"

"Oh Jane. I'm so glad you answered. I barely remembered the numbers to push."

"Algernon? Are you alright?"

"No, I'm not, if you must know. They have detained me overnight in the most hellish place I've ever been. I cannot even begin to explain the people I have encountered, nor do I wish to sully your delicate ears. I was allowed a call to one person. They say I'm free to go. Could you please come rescue me post haste?

"Wait, of course, but where are you? Did you say detained?"

"Yes, I'm mortified, and enraged. But they have dared to place me in some sort of prison."

She gasped. "I'll be there straight away."

He was able to give her the address with the help of an officer standing by, and she called Charles. "Might I have the use of your driver? It's an emergency."

"Going to bust your boyfriend out of prison?"

"What? How could you know that?"

"It's all over the news, the papers, the websites, everyone is talking about the royal tiff at Layton's Club last night."

"Oh no. Can I have the car?"

"Certainly, I'll come with you. Be there in ten minutes."

The enactment was almost complete. She hoped he won. He would find the research as fascinating as she, and it disproved his theory that women were useless. Perhaps it could convince him to focus on other directions for his work.

She waited on the front steps, and when the car pulled up

she was at the door before the driver could exit and open it for her.

Charles rolled down a window and winked. When she opened the door and sat inside, Charles pulled her into an embrace. He looked delicious. She couldn't help but notice. Back in his Regency attire. "We're getting ready for the ball."

"Do you have time to take me?"

"Certainly. It is far easier to get ready as a male for these parties than it is for the women. Unless you're Beau Brummel."

"He was ridiculous, though, and famous for it." She laughed. "I would like to have met him. I heard it took him close to six hours to dress."

"I've read the same."

Jane sat back against the seat, anxious to arrive at the prison. "So, what happened? What is the press saying?"

"He and Baron Smithing got in a brawl, a regular fistfight over Lady Anna. Apparently His Grace was getting too close to her ladyship and the baron didn't like it, so he popped him a hard one, right in the eye. His Grace took to swinging, shouting something about Jackson's Club being too far away and they were soon at it so hot and heavy the security was called and the police brought in. It's an automatic overnight stay for brawling in public, with a phone call in the morning. No one pressed charges, but the other nobles deserted him. Lord Smithing got out without his stay overnight, but no one would speak for Algernon."

"This is terrible. He's going to want to go home for sure now."

"Home? Does he not live here in England?"

She realized her mistake. "Yes, of course. I just mean, he's going to want to go back there. He's from the Brighton area."

She whipped out the first name far from their location that popped into her head.

"No matter where he is in England, this is going to haunt him. Paparazzi, press, pundits, onions. He'd best leave the country."

That suited Jane just fine, except for the gala. She'd hoped to gather some support for her fundraiser, but Charles could help maybe. "I could use your help with something else."

He leaned forward. "How can I be of service?"

She detailed her fund-raising plans, the event she hoped to plan and her desire to use the gala to find more people who might support her from England. "Might you do some of that legwork for me, find some additional support?"

"I might."

She eyed him. "What can I do for you in return?"

"It's a matter of the research."

"Won't you be able to see it also? Surely you will win?"

He rubbed a smudge on his shiny hessians with his thumb. "I'm certain I will, but the prize doesn't include it all. I will be shown a select few pieces, where I am guessing you had access to all of it."

"Mmm, true." She thought of the references to time travel, the letters to Algernon. Some of it she could never reveal. "I will give you a much broader access than you will get."

"When?"

"Come to New York. There. You can have access to all my digital copies."

"Done. I'll bring you a team the ladies will drool over, and you will share your research." He raised an eyebrow. "Shall we shake on it?"

She held out her hand.

"There was a time I had hoped for more than a handshake from you. We could have been a powerhouse couple."

"True." If he didn't totally disagreed with the direction of her research, if his own opinions of women didn't make her ill. But at least he was handsome, and he was helping her, and that meant a lot. "But I hope we can be friends?"

"Friends. Allies even." They shook.

"Thank you for your help."

They pulled up to an older-looking building, and Jane already felt ill just thinking about Algernon in there overnight. "Oh boy."

"Let's go break your boyfriend out of jail." He placed a hand at the small of her back. "That sentence alone should give you pause about dating this fellow. Have you ever considered he could be a fraud? He shows up totally wasted, leaning against a wall, mostly unresponsive. How realistic is it that no one knew of his heritage, that he himself didn't know until now?"

"Well, if you consider his family and estate broke apart over one hundred years ago, it's pretty realistic that they would all be lost and unaware of their heritage. But his nearly identical resemblance to the 1817 Duke is quite remarkable."

Charles grunted. "Here we go." He held open the door and they entered a musty, dark entry.

The lady behind a glass partition eyed them without a greeting, but her eyes traveled up and down the length of Charles more than once.

Jane hid her grin as she approached and spoke through three holes in the glass. "We are here to pick up Algernon Ramsbury."

"Ah, the duke. Yes, just a moment."

She picked up a telephone and had a conversation before

speaking again to Jane. "They're bringing him out. I see you have a car. You may want some security backup."

"Why?" Jane turned back to peer outside. A small window in the doorway revealed Charles's car surrounded by people with cameras, even the large TV-looking cameras. "Oh no. What do we do?"

Charles shrugged. "I guess we go out in that mess and get in the car and try to lose them."

The lady frowned. "I don't recommend it without security detail."

Jane scoffed. "Can't someone from inside help us? This is the police station, right?"

The clerk behind the glass looked down her nose. "It's the prison, and everyone inside is busy doing their job."

"I understand that, but we don't have security detail."

Charles held up his hand and made a call. "I'll take care of it."

Within a few minutes, men in suit coats showed up and parted a way in the crowd.

Algernon was brought out through a pair of metallic double doors, and Jane resisted the urge to rush to him, throwing arms around his back.

He looked from her to Charles and back, and then Charles said, "Come on, we've got to get you out through this mess and into the car."

They rushed out the door, and people pushed toward them, shouting questions, making accusations. "Who looks worse, you or the baron?"

"Was she worth it?"

"That's what you get for stealing someone's girlfriend."

News cameras were filming, and Jane didn't know what

else to do but hurry to the car. They climbed in. The doors shut, and the car pulled away.

She turned to Algernon, wishing Charles wasn't present so they could talk more openly. "What happened?"

"I will tell you all once we are alone."

Charles hmphed. "There's nothing you are about to say that I haven't already seen on the internet."

"What's the—"

Jane kicked him. "You're all over the papers, the press, the news, the gossip."

He nodded. "I am mortified by my behavior. The only excuse I have are the five cups of brandy I drank before we started dancing."

"Did you really punch him? In the eye?"

"I think so. It's all rather blurry, to be honest. I tell you, I was not in my right mind, not thinking clearly. And he hit me first." Algernon indicated the slight purplish color around his left eye.

"Well, that excuses everything, then." She turned away, angry they were even having this conversation.

Charles crossed his arms. "And Lady Anna?"

"What about her?" Algernon's possessive tone was enough for Jane to know something more existed between them.

"I see." She cleared her throat. "Charles thinks you will be hounded by the press for weeks on end and it would be advised to leave the country as soon as possible."

He rubbed a hand down his face. "That is convenient, since we were hoping to go to America, were we not?"

Charles raised an eyebrow.

Jane nodded. "Yes, but I think we should skip the gala and leave straightaway if you're okay with that."

"I care not to see any of them ever again. They left me, you know. You didn't see any of them spending the night in such a place."

"I know. I wish I'd known. I'm sorry Algernon."

He reached for her hand, but she moved aside. So he returned his hand to his lap. "Thank you for coming today."

"You're welcome. I'm just grateful Charles came too. For the car and for his security team." She turned to him. "Speaking of, how did you—"

He waved her question aside. "A needed asset at times."

Algernon nodded to him. "Impressive show of force. It's as if you have your own team of footmen who follow you about."

"You'll find in our day, we commoners have resources too." She couldn't help it. Now that he was back in front of her, his earlier snub and snobbish comments were beginning to rankle anew.

"Commoner?" Charles widened his eyes. "Am I to be a commoner now?"

"No, it's just something ridiculous Algernon and I were talking about. How there are so few nobles in the world and that nowadays people can actually become much more than they ever could where he's from." She stopped and wanted to bite her tongue.

Charles squinted his eyes. "You talk as if he's really from the past, as though he were raised in the 1800s." He scoffed. "You do know he's a normal dude, a man just like the rest of us?"

She felt her face heat. Somehow she'd have to stop making rash comments. "Yes, of course. But come to think of it. You're not much of a commoner, are you?"

He shrugged and at once looked a mite self-deprecating. "I'm not, actually, but I'd prefer if you continued to think of me as such."

She didn't push it for now, but planned to Google the heck

out of him later. Charles looked behind them. "Looks as though the last straggler has given up following you. But I would guess that by tomorrow morning the enactment at Twickenham will be crawling with reporters. Hopefully that Nellie woman appreciates the free press she's about to get."

"Do you think they'll find us at Lichfield?"

"I suggest you be gone by then."

Jane nodded. "Excellent. Algernon. It's time you learned to fly on an airplane."

"He doesn't know how to fly on an airplane?" Charles's incredulous look told Jane it might be better if she stopped talking altogether.

"Air sick."

He rolled his eyes. The car stopped in front of Chatwick Manor, and Jane and Algernon rushed inside. She called over her shoulder. "Thank you, Charles, for everything. I'll be in touch."

He waved and then she ran up the steps and closed the door behind Algernon.

As soon as they were inside, Lady Anna's silky voice called from the front drawing room. "There you are, darling. Come in here so I can see to your injuries."

Algernon winked at Jane. "Once you see to our travel preparations, I'll be ready to go. Come fetch me."

"And Jane!"

Her voice grated every last nerve in Jane's body.

"Don't worry, I've got a passport and identification for him."

Jane almost screamed in frustration. She was not his servant, nor his travel agent. And he seemed to think doing his bidding her new place in his life. Anna also. She dug around in her purse, looking for her phone to change her flight reservation and add him to hers. It wasn't cheap to fly internationally, and especially not last minute. But she made the changes and went upstairs to pack her things. Algernon could pack his own things as far as she was concerned.

Once she'd lugged the huge trunk down the stairs, one loud thunk at a time, she waited in the foyer, unsure how to spend her time. She thought one last visit to their research room would be enjoyable. What an incredible experience. How many people had a find such as the one she'd had? She couldn't wait to start going through the data and continuing with her thesis.

As she reached for her keys, her hands grazed the envelope Nellie had given her. She hadn't quite forgotten it, but had successfully pushed it away every time the thought tried to get her attention. She frowned. He could stay here and go back home in two weeks. She hesitated.

All his arrogant comments, his dallying with Lady Anna even now in the other room—suddenly two weeks seemed a fair trade. He couldn't leave yet anyway, so a trip to help her in America in the meantime seemed just the thing. He didn't care, so she wouldn't either. No. She would tell him how to get home when she was good and ready. It's not like it mattered. He was traveling through time. He could go back to whatever time he wanted, like he'd never left. As far as she was concerned, he had all the time in the world.

# CHAPTER 15

*T*he airplane landed, and Algernon let go of Jane's hand, not because he wanted to but because she seemed a bit bristly about him reaching for her. She probably allowed his hand squeezing hers in such a panicked manner because his terror was obvious. Certain the pilot would send them crashing to earth, his breathing had picked up. Perspiration lined his forehead, and he had reached for her and gripped her hand as though it would stop him from falling from the sky.

Now that they had stopped moving, he waited for his heart to calm and stared out the window, as though to prove he had once again returned to the ground.

Ever since she picked him up from prison, she'd seemed cold, distant. He didn't blame her. Who maintained respect for a man who needed rescuing from the local magistrate? Though he still couldn't believe the audacity. Who arrests a duke? Even though Jane had explained it to him several times, he didn't understand a system where the nobles weren't respected, revered. Were they not of certain families, born to rule? He had always been under the impression they had a certain intelligence, gifts that rendered them superior. But now, meeting Jane, who seemed far more intelligent than most people he knew, he wasn't sure what to think about his birthright.

He flexed his fingers. Flying scared him out of his mind, but as he had stared out over the ocean and watched it pass beneath him, he couldn't fathom the many inventions a human was capable of. If someone could create a machine that would fly, there was no end to what more they could invent. He determined to find those minds of a particular aptitude and support their efforts. In his time.

At last they stood and filed out of the plane. Jane touched the first seat at the front of the plane with her fingers. He followed the flutters of her soft fingertips as she outlined the seat number. 1A. They passed the cockpit. He had lingered there when they boarded, the flight attendants pointing out instruments until the pilot arrived and told him to find his seat. Fascinating.

Jane walked a few steps to his front, never quite allowing him to catch up. She'd taken to wearing pants now. As much as he enjoyed the familiarity of the morning dress, he loved her in pants.

"Would you just wait a moment?"

She turned, impatience sparkling out of her eyes. "Excuse me?"

"You won't walk beside me. You won't talk to me. Please, Jane, I miss your hand on my arm." He grinned his most charming smile, at least he thought it was charming. Women had always responded as if it was, but Jane just turned and huffed out a breath of air.

"If you want to walk beside me, keep up. In New York, people move."

He looked around. "Yes, and no one looks any happier because of it."

A man tried to shove past him but rammed into Algernon's unmoving side. The man grunted, frowned, and then moved on.

"Is everyone in America rude and miserable?"

Her eyes softened for a moment, and she slowed to walk beside him. "No, but just about everyone in this airport appears to be, don't they?"

Pleased to have her again at his side, he asked, "Have I ruined what we once had between us?"

She looked away. "Can't we just get home first? Now is not really the time for a big discussion."

"I see no better time."

They exited out into a rainy, dark, and dreary day. The wind whipped through his clothes as though he weren't wearing any. "I feel we have happened upon the perfect weather for your mood."

She scowled at him.

"Why this morose face? What weather would you use to describe your mood? Sunny? Warm and breezy with just a touch of rose in the air?" He winked, hoping she would warm to him.

"Algernon. I'm sorry we commoners are unable to meet your every need, including our mood, but some of us have work that needs to get done, including finding a cab home."

"Can we not just enter one of these waiting carriages? Cars?" His hand indicated the row of yellow parked cars.

"Yes, precisely." She walked toward one, Algernon behind, pushing the cart with their trunks.

As soon as they were packed in, Jane sitting in front, Algernon in the back next to one of the trunks, the cab headed away from the airport and through the city.

"What is that?" They approached a towering structure that appeared to open up into the air around it, huge drop offs on either side.

"That is a huge bridge."

Algernon couldn't fathom something of that magnitude spanned over water. "Are we certain it's quite safe?"

Jane shared a look with the driver. "We're certain."

He felt his stomach drop when their car went up on the bridge. What was wrong with him? He told himself to gain a backbone. Yes, the future was different; he must adjust.

The longer they drove, the more Algernon felt as though he had not only left his time but his world also. He craned his neck and still could not see the tops of the buildings around him. "I'm sorry Jane, but is there no greenery any more in this country?"

She sighed. "There's greenery. Where we're going there are a few trees outside on the sidewalk."

A few trees. He was aghast.

"And a large park, similar to Hyde Park, where people gather and promenade and get a bit of the weather."

He looked outside his window at the pelting rain.

"London isn't any better, if you recall."

He cringed at the reminder of his activities in London. "I recall. Detestable place."

People. Everywhere. They weren't quite promenading, more like pushing through to get somewhere in the utmost haste. With frowns. They stopped at a light. A man huddled under a tiny alcove against the rain. "Do people live out on the street? Out here in the open?"

Jane turned to him. "You cannot pretend that the poor had it any better where you're from."

He thought of the parts of London he would not go to, of the undesirables, the filth of society. Watching a man now, leaning up against the brick wall, dirt streaking down his face and his eyes, hollow, unseeing, Algernon wondered if he might perhaps do more for those others he had for so long tried to avoid.

They stopped in front of a towering gray building.

"We're here."

He stared up at the falling rain. Jane got out of the car and started pulling her trunk from the back. She slapped his window. "Come on, no footmen here."

He stepped into the rain, yanking out his trunk and putting it up on a shoulder like he'd seen a particularly broad footman do. "Bring that inside and I'll take it up the rest of the way."

He enjoyed Jane's open mouth of astonishment. So, she thought him incapable, a dandy of some sort? Well, he could show her a different side.

She jerked and yanked hers up the stairs and inside the door that he held open. Then he lowered his trunk to the floor, rotating his shoulders. "Tell me you have one of those fabulous rising boxes here."

"Elevators?" She laughed. "Yes, we have one of those."

He hefted her trunk and motioned with his hand. "Show the way. I'll be back down for the other one."

She pushed the button, then hurried back to his trunk and shoved it along the floor. Literally almost on her hands and knees she was pushing the heavy beast all the way to him. When the elevator arrived, she slid it forward after him.

"Ah, ingenious. We shall all ride up together with our things." The place smelled of something a bit sour with a hint of spice. A cacophony of smells assaulted his nose. It reminded him a bit of the docks, but there the smells mixed with the salt of the sea and the fresh air all around. However, these smells were old, musty, and dank.

"Home sweet home." Jane smiled. "It's gonna be different from what you're used to." Instead of nervous or embarrassed, her expression held a hint of challenge.

He stood taller. "Jane, thank you. Where would I go, if not here? You have given a truly homeless man a place to lie his head, and I'm thankful."

Her face softened, and he thought that perhaps he had broken back in to a portion of her good graces.

They at last made it to her door. And entered to one of the most charming spaces he had ever seen. The apartment boasted full windows. She lived up high in the building and had a lovely view over rooftops to a green area. The seating arrangement was comfortable, inviting. And the smell, lovely. Nothing more of the assault from the hallway. Her rooms smelled clean, fresh, and warm, almost as though a cook had just baked something delicious. Without restraint, his mouth turned up into a smile.

"What?" Jane laughed. "You look as though you just won the —a prize."

"I did. Utterly charming. Your home is lovely."

Her cheeks flamed red. And he was happy to affect her so. "Where would you like me to take the trunks?"

"I have a bit of an office space down this hallway. You can put your trunk in there, and mine goes in my bedroom at the end of the hall." She led the way. "Algernon. While you're here, we're going to have to figure out a bed for you. I obviously wasn't expecting you . . ."

"Whatever we figure out will be just fine with me. And if

you need me to look elsewhere, I can do that as well." Though he hoped to stay as close as he could to Jane. Even if she was unhappy with him, he still felt inexplicably drawn to her and unsure how to even get around in this new place without her.

"No, stay here." She laughed. "I mean, if you want to go elsewhere, you are welcome to, but I'd really like it if you were here, with me. In your own bed."

He felt his own cheeks warm. "Of course, naturally, I would never think otherwise." He tilted his head, considering. "You don't have anyone else living here, no staff, no chaperones . . ."

She shook her head. "No. It's pretty common in our day. To live alone. I prefer it to a bunch of roommates. Though I'm happy to have you as a roommate. That's not what I mean."

He nodded slowly. "And your reputation. When others discover our situation?"

"We can explain how perfectly platonic we are, friends, roommates. It will fly just fine, I should think. Though my parents might wonder. Perhaps we should keep it from my parents. If you ever meet them. My office staff. They're going to go crazy."

He held up his hands. "So some will think this is perfectly acceptable and others might question your reputation?"

She hesitated and then nodded. "But I'm fine with that."

"The people you most respect, what will they think?"

She avoided his eyes. And then a moment of clarity filled her face. "They will listen to my explanation and respect my choices. Unless they're my parents, and those two will make all kinds of assumptions I would rather they not make."

He stepped closer. "These assumptions, about us not simply being friends." He took her hand in his.

She nodded.

"And will they be correct in assuming something more than

friendship exists between us?" He stepped as close to her as he dared.

She didn't answer, but the nervous flutter of her eyelashes empowered him to be bold, to wipe the insecurity from her mind. Her face tilted up, and he met her eyes. They were bare, unsure, questioning. He began, "From the moment I met you, I've considered you to be a friend, yes."

She looked away.

He rested a hand at the side of her face, hoping she would return his gaze once again. "Meaning I felt I could trust you, but that trust has grown to much more. I can't be near you without wanting to be closer. When we are apart, I want us to be together. When you are silent, I try to guess your thoughts, and when you speak, I drink in every word. We are friends, but you, Jane, have taken over my every desire as your own."

She swallowed, and then her eyes teared up. "You, you don't find me common?"

He lifted one side of his mouth. "Nothing about you is common. I find every detail most extraordinary." He caressed the side of her face. "And I want nothing more than to press my lips to yours and never stop." He kissed one cheek. Then the other. "But here we are alone and plan to be so for hours on end."

She nodded again.

"And so perhaps I shall forbear." He kissed her forehead. "And remain the gentleman I call myself."

Jane huffed out her breath. "So, never? You will never kiss me?" Her cheeks flushed. "I mean, that's fine if you don't want to."

"Outside the apartment. Perhaps an opportune moment will arise in a more likely place."

She stared back into his face, searching his eyes, his mouth, his jawline. He felt her gaze as a caress on his skin and resisted pulling her up against him, but only just. Then she stepped back but held onto his hand. "How about a tour of your new space?"

# CHAPTER 16

They grabbed blankets and a pillow and made a makeshift bed for Algernon on her couch. She couldn't believe her Regency man was here in New York, sleeping in her living room. The sleeping in her living room part was going to take some getting used to. She knew it wasn't permanent, and she tried to put that thought aside. The envelope in her bag was boring a hole in her thoughts. But in the meantime, how would she even sleep? His almost kiss had her distracted still. She was aware of every shift of his body. And now that he'd changed into a pair of athletic shorts and a T-shirt, he just seemed so approachable, so much a part of her world, she was having a hard time not initiating something. Reminding her of his previous pompous behavior did nothing to douse the attraction.

So to distract herself, she rummaged through the kitchen for some ice cream and Oreos. "You are in for a treat."

"Am I?"

"Oh, most certainly." She sat beside him and thrilled as the length of his thigh pressed against hers. She handed him a spoon. "Here. Take a bite." She held out the ice cream, cookies and cream flavor.

He pressed his spoon in, grabbing the carton with one hand so that he could exert more effort, then he put a bit on his tongue. And closed his eyes. And his moaning almost made her swoon like a true Regency lady. "This is delectable. What do you call this?"

"Um." She watched him lick his spoon, almost forgetting the question. "Ice cream."

She took a bite with her spoon and then handed it back to him for his turn, scooting closer.

He dipped his spoon but this time offered it to her and watched as her mouth closed around it. He eyed her lips until she swallowed. She licked her lips, full of crazy desire, and watched him. When their eyes met, no one bothered to hide anything. He took another small bit on his spoon and spread it along her lower lip and then watched as she ran her tongue along its sweetness. He did it again, this time kissing it off, softly, gently. She swallowed, opened her mouth slightly. He reached for the carton and her spoon and placed them on the table. His arm wrapped around her back, pulled her close and captured her lips with his own. She melted against him. Everything about him overwhelmed her, his mouth on hers was no exception. She responded with as much enthusiasm as she felt until he pushed away. "No, oh Jane, I'm sorry. I quite forgot myself."

"Sorry? What? No. No, don't worry about that here, Algernon. If I want to kiss and you want to kiss, people just kiss."

He stared. "And no one thinks anything untoward?"

"Not at all." She pulled him closer. She didn't dare tell him what else everyone did, because she was very conservative in her actions with men, but she was a rarity among her friends.

He wrapped one arm around her and used the other to keep them upright. "Jane." He mumbled against her mouth. Then he separated and leaned back against his seat on the couch. "You. Are. Magnificent." His grin widened. "We shall make use of this new freedom as often as possible."

When she leaned back toward him, seeking the softness of his lips again on her own, he held up a hand. "But for now, let's desist for a time. I'm afraid I'm overwhelmed at the moment."

"Oh, okay. Um, try this treat too." She handed him an Oreo. "It's best when dipped in the ice cream."

He took a bite but winced. "Good heavens that is sweet." He blinked twice and then put the Oreo back down on the table.

She went to grab blankets and a pillow. Once he had everything he needed, she sat on the chair opposite his couch and said, "Can we talk?"

He leaned forward, hands on his knees. "Certainly, my lady." His smile let her know he knew how much she enjoyed their Regency pretend speak.

"While we were at your home, I got a phone call with some disturbing news."

His eyes softened. "I'm sorry to hear it."

"Remember I told you my work researches the times in which you live. And, well, we've lost all our funding and they are threatening to close the whole office unless my research provides something unique, and also unless I can find a way to bring in more money."

"Your research should be amazingly useful."

"Yes, I'm going to do my best with this dissertation, my paper, so that we have plenty of new and unique research coming out of the society."

"And?"

"And, I have an idea of a way to bring in more funds." She

wasn't sure what he would think of her idea. But she took a deep breath and asked anyway. "I want to have a Regency Man in Breeches auction."

"Pardon me?"

"I was hoping you would participate and I would re-create an evening at a typical Regency ball and we would have authentic costumes and everything and at the beginning of the night we would auction off the men—the women would get them for a date through the evening and for a night on the town afterward."

He shifted, obviously uncomfortable. "So you would like me to present myself up for sale? What is involved in this night on the town?"

"Nothing untoward. This sort of thing happens quite a bit in our day. It's all in good fun and often earns quite a bit of money, depending on who we invite. So the idea would be that Charles would bring some of the other men of title from England."

He stood up, "What, like Lord Smithing? You know I cannot abide him."

"I know, but you don't have to abide him. Some woman would have to abide him. You would just need to be available for one evening." She sat back, eyes wide, hoping. She could hold the auction without him, but she did need every man in breeches she could find, and she wasn't biased when she admitted that he was the best looking one of any she'd seen. "We are asking for the men from the reenactment as well as others I know here in America."

"What exactly do we do during this auction?"

"We would read a bio about you, tell what you like and don't like, where you're from and something interesting about you, and you would perhaps turn in place, you might walk across the front a few times."

"You want me to parade about in the front of the room so that women might bid on me? I am trying not to be completely humiliated by the prospect. You say this is done? It's not . . . because I will admit it seems . . . I hate to bring up such a subject in the presence of a lady, but—"

"Yes, I know what it sounds like, but I promise it isn't. It's simply a fun way to earn a bunch of money for my work."

"I'll think about it. I'm not looking forward to presenting myself like a piece of horseflesh at Tattersalls."

"Thank you." She stood. "Oh and also, I'm taking you to work tomorrow if you don't mind. We have a whole lot of work to do for my research."

"It would be my pleasure."

"And the women. They're going to be all over you."

"Are there any men? At your work?"

"Just one, and you probably won't see him."

"Hmm. Interesting." His mouth quirked up in what she could only describe as a wicked grin. "All over me how?"

"Oh stop. They are all going to love you. So if you want a fun American girlfriend . . ."

"Girlfriend. What is this?"

"Oh, right. Sort of like someone you're courting but you may not be thinking about marriage yet, you just spend a lot of time together, and you only have one girlfriend at a time."

"So, like you're courting but you could stop courting the woman and no irreparable damage would be made to her reputation."

"Yes, exactly. Though usually when relationships end, both people are sad."

He sat quietly for so long she considered standing and

calling it a night. But then he said, "How long must you see a girl before she becomes your girlfriend?" His eyes watched her even more intensely than usual.

"There is no set time for things like that. Some people know right away that they want to keep seeing each other, and some couples don't decide to be exclusive until after they've known each other for a long time."

"And what if a person wants to become a boyfriend to a girl? What should he do?"

"Well, you'd have to start acting like you're interested, doing nice things for her, going out on dates—"

"Living in her apartment?"

She laughed. "Well yes, some people do that, but . . ."

He started laughing. "I'm teasing you. I'm sorry. I guess I hope to make this less uncomfortable for you. Are you sure it won't damage your reputation?"

"I'm certain we will be fine." She stood and walked by his couch. "Good night, Algernon."

He reached for her hand and caressed it in his own. Then he placed his lips in the center of her palm. "Good night, Lady Sullivan."

"Your Grace," she whispered, shivers running up her arm from the lingering feel of his lips.

"And Jane?"

"Yes?"

"I'd like to be your boyfriend."

Her heart thumped. She wanted so badly to be his girl-friend. "Let's talk about it in the morning. You won't be here forever."

"All the more reason to enjoy the time we have. If you say its purpose is not to lead to marriage, we might enjoy ourselves, no?"

150

Confusion filled her. She knew what he was asking, like a summer fling kind of thing, but she didn't think her heart could take it. Already she was priming herself for a huge break when he had to leave. But if they started getting serious, she might never tell him how to get home, and when he found out, he'd hate her and leave anyway. "Let's talk about it later. Good night, Algernon."

When she closed her bedroom door and thought of him so close on the other side, she didn't know how she could possibly ever sleep again.

# CHAPTER 17

*A*lgernon woke up to the smell of breakfast and sounds in the kitchen. Her staff must come in during the early hours of the morning. He would have to commend them, for he heard not even a footstep. He stretched and made his way into the kitchen.

What he saw astounded him. Jane danced, holding some form of kitchen device in her hand, shook her hips, and bounced up and down on her bare feet. He eyed her slender ankles, her form-fitting pants, and her tight shirt and was at a loss. He was equally enticed and shocked that he could see so much of her all at once. And he absolutely wanted to take her up into his arms and kiss her good morning.

He stepped up behind her and starting mimicking her moves, laughing to himself. She seemed to be listening to something he couldn't hear. Her ears had small white things in them. He would never tire of all the new modern inventions in her day. And he would never again be able to appreciate the dress of women in his day. Jane looked more enticing than he'd ever seen her.

She wiggled in a circle and stopped when she saw him. Her face turned the bright pink of the embarrassed, and he found her more charming than ever. She recovered quickly and grabbed his hand to keep up their dance a moment more. Then she waved him over to the table. "Breakfast is ready."

He waited until she sat beside him and then she showed him how to pour a sticky brown liquid on top of what she called pancakes, to cut them with his fork, and eat. As he chewed his first bite, he groaned again. "This is as good as ice cream."

"No."

"It is. I could eat this all day, what is this sticky substance?"

"Syrup, maple syrup."

"It is the perfect food. Perhaps it pairs well with others?"

"I don't know. I only usually eat it with these types of breakfast foods, pancakes, French toast, those kinds." She watched with widened eyes as he dumped more syrup on his dish.

She took her own bite and smiled. "It really is quite good. You know, it comes from a tree, a sugar maple. I wonder if they have them in England." She clicked on her phone. "Siri, do sugar maples grow in England?"

"This is what I found on the web for 'do sugar maples grow in England?'"

She touched her phone a couple times and then showed him. "Look. The first sugar maple showed up in England in 1705. You could find some and make your own syrup."

If he were to ever get home again. Algernon didn't mention it much to Jane, but he was growing more and more concerned about his estate. Perhaps Nellie was correct, no one would even know he was gone, but knowing that he was the cause of an entire estate going to ruin, a family being disbursed and forgotten—it didn't sit well with him, and if he allowed his mind to linger on the thought, it was all he could do to not go running back to Nellie and demand a return. He assumed he could get back. He wasn't sure exactly how it worked, but Nellie was the key. He knew that much.

He and Jane rode the subway into her work. It was stuffy, smelled abominably, and was filled with people of questionable appearance and countenance. He was pressed against on all sides by people who refused to meet his eyes. "So, this subway, it is a preferred method of travel for you?"

Jane swayed when the subway slowed to make a stop. She stood on tiptoes to speak quietly in his ear. "Perhaps we should save our conversation for when we arrive?" She glanced at those around them.

His eyes flitted to the people nearby also, none too friendly. Then he nodded. But he couldn't keep quiet. "I feel that if someone is to spend such a large amount of time in a conveyance it ought to have some semblance of enjoyment, should it not?"

The lady near him smirked.

"See, now this lovely lady here. We have not been introduced, so I am sure this will seem very untoward of me, but perhaps if she and I conversed, the journey might be all the more pleasurable." He winked and felt rewarded that her cheeks colored.

Then she turned from him and pulled out her phone.

"And you sir—" Algernon turned to a man pressed up against him, sharing the same pole to keep his balance.

The tall bald head shone from the dim lights overhead. "Keep your opinions to yourself."

"Understood." How strange to share the same space so closely and have nothing to say to one another.

Then a man standing as tall as Algernon nodded to him over the tops of the all the others. He wore a handkerchief on his head, all black, a thick jacket of sorts, leather. He carried chains around his neck. Algernon was at first repulsed by the hair that bushed out underneath the handkerchief on the man's head, and covered his face and neck. But the man smiled. And Algernon could appreciate the effort to reach out. Then the man said, "You from England?"

Algernon nodded, and the man next to him closed his eyes, with seeming great forbearance. "I am. New to this city."

"Welcome. I remember my first day in the city, my first subway. It's something."

Algernon laughed. "Nothing like I've ever experienced." Most passengers tried to act like they weren't listening, but there was nothing else of import in the otherwise silent train, so they heard it all.

"We have a group. Get together on Thursdays. We always welcome a Brit. Call me." His long arm stretched a hand across the heads of those in between them and handed Algernon his card, and the gesture warmed him. "Thank you." He nodded. And suddenly felt as though Beau Brummel himself had left his card. "I will." He pocketed the card.

Jane stood on her toes to speak in his ear. Her breath tickled his neck, and he wished to wrap her in his arms. She warned, "Perhaps it's best if we just ride in silence."

Soon the doors opened to their stop. People shoved forward and, whether he was ready or not, they were now all standing outside the subway car. The doors closed, and it took off again down the dark path. As soon as they stepped out onto the platform, Algernon reached for Jane's hand.

Before he could say anything, she huffed. "What are you

doing talking to people on the subway? And why take that man's card? You're not going to go hang out with him."

Algernon frowned. "He was the one shining star amidst the bleakness. What is wrong with people in America?"

"He looked like he carried multiple knives." She shook her head. "It's not really America. It's more New York City, more the subway, really."

"What a detestable place."

"I'm sorry it's not up to your standards of travel, but it's all we have right now. There are other manners of arriving at work, none of which I can pay for." Her eyes flashed, and he knew he'd reminded her of the whole difference in class between them.

"Jane, no, it isn't that. I just think that no matter the conveyance it's made all the more pleasurable if inhabited by delightful people. That lot were not delightful, except for my new friend." He pulled out his card. "Says he's a member of the brotherhood. Look here, what's this?"

She glanced. "It's a motorcycle. He's part of a biker gang. All the more reason to steer clear."

"I don't know, I liked him. He was the only pleasant person . . . except for the one woman. She seemed pleasant enough."

Jane just pushed forward, and he picked up his pace after her.

They had arrived at an older building when a voice called to Algernon. "Your Grace!"

He turned. Lady Anna waved at him, a group following.

"I've found you. How fortunate." She kissed his cheeks and smiled in such a happy way, he could only grin in response.

"Hello. You see I'm still out of prison and far away from your newspapers." He eyed her, clear to express his displeasure for being deserted. He had not forgotten her abandonment, even though she'd aided him in finding a passport. "Thanks to Jane."

"Yes, and you're repaying her splendidly by helping with her research, no doubt."

He didn't answer. Jane came to stand beside him. "Algernon?"

"I'll be in, in a minute."

Lady Anna waved her hand in farewell. "Yes, yes, of course, go off to your work, but here." She held out a small gray device. "I've purchased a cell phone for you. As soon as you left, I had no way to be in touch. A group of us came, supporting Jane's auction. She's created quite the stir with her friend Charles. It's all the buzz over there and soon will be here, I'm sure."

"Thank you." He turned to follow Jane into the building, calling ahead to her retreating form. "That's good news, right? All the support for your event?"

"Yes, of course." She paused to wait for him. "I don't know if I trust her, but for now, I'm thrilled. Charles must have really talked it up. I'll have to call him tonight."

Algernon wanted to find some sort of fault with Charles, but he couldn't. They entered a narrow hall and climbed a set of stairs at the back. When they entered what must be her offices, everyone went quiet. He looked down to ensure his presentability and then dipped his head in a small bow to the room.

The buzz of their conversation began again. Jane's smile was small, unsurprised. So he followed her direction and made no comment.

She led him to a larger space with a table in the middle of the room. Another woman entered and squealed and hugged Jane.

"This is Chelsea. She runs the society. We're gonna be working with her on this event and on the research."

He took her hand, bowed over it, and placed the whisper of a kiss on her knuckles. She seemed a good sort of person, and Jane obviously cared for her.

She fanned her face. "Wow, if they're all like him, we're gonna make bank."

Jane's eyes turned wistful. "No one is quite like Algernon. But we will have men of title and reenactment experts. We've got an excellent group coming. We just need to plan this thing, excellent venue, tickets top dollar, black tie event."

"On it. I already have a team working on the details. They're negotiating with a venue as we speak."

"Can we use the conference room for a few days? I'd like to touch base with Algernon about the research, organize it, and hear from him firsthand about his experiences."

"Absolutely. I'm going to make some phone calls, and I'll be back in to hear more about what you discovered."

He and Jane sat in chairs at the head of the table. Algernon watched her eyes light up when she pulled images up on the far screen. "You haven't told me yet," he said, "what it is you discovered."

"So many things, a couple I'm not sure what to make of. First, my original premise was true, about the women. Surely there were strong independent women in your day. And I had hoped the letters and documents from this one family of sisters who never married could help prove that theory." She paused, eyebrows raised.

"While I'd never want to disavow any theory of yours, I will add, one of my many frustrations with women of my day is their inability to take a stand on any issue, even something as benign as the weather. They simper and primp and try to please, all the while never giving even a hint of the kind of person behind all the niceties."

"Except the ladies at Chatwick Manor. You behaved differently with them."

"True, but that stemmed from childhood acquaintance. Some things continued through the years. But those women. I would never call them simpering or anything like it. If I had, I was likely to get hit in the head with a mud ball."

Jane laughed, and Algernon enjoyed the sound.

"That's what I'm trying to prove. Not all women were as you describe, perhaps those were just the faces they portray at Almack's." She clicked ahead a couple images to a letter. Algernon recognized the handwriting at once. She enlarged the image. "But that's not all I hope to discuss in my work."

She read, "My dearest Algernon . . ." The face she turned to him was full of questions. "It was never sent. She declares long and ardent love for you over and again . . . and discusses a time in the future when she hopes you two can be together."

This was the first Algernon had ever heard of it, but Lady Bethany, if it was her, could very well have long admired him. They played together as children splendidly well, but those visits tapered off, and then he was off to school. He had rarely thought of her since.

"Look at how she writes the word *future*. The handwriting changes and looks almost modern there, you see that?"

He looked closer. "I do see a change, but I confess I don't know what modern writing looks like."

Jane waved her hand. "That's all fine. But look, see the signature. Lady Anna . . . which is it? Bethany or Anna? Do you suppose . . ."

"It's her, Jane. I suspect the Lady Anna that you know here and this Lady Anna of my past are one and the same. I called her Bethany there, a middle name, but she went by Anna. She spoke of it last week, though it was hard to tell. She could have been speaking as a descendant only."

"Well, does she look like her? Could it be her?"

"I don't know. She dresses so differently, behaves differently, has all that makeup on her face. I haven't seen her in years. It is difficult to tell, to be honest." He cleared his throat. "And perhaps I never looked closely at her face anyway. We were too busy playing."

"And the portrait?"

"The one with the secret note? I don't know. I didn't sit for it. I have no idea as to its meaning. Perhaps it is from a time yet to be?"

Jane frowned in concentration. "And the woman? Is it meant to be Anna?" She pulled out her book, well worn. It opened onto the page as it always did.

Algernon turned to her, a hopeful expression on his face. "Do you study it often?"

She looked away and then seemed to give up her resistance. "I used to look at it every day. You were my example of the perfect Regency man. I know it sounds silly, but I've been intrigued by the questions in this portrait for years."

He pulled it closer. "I am a far cry from the perfect Regency man. I am about to destroy generations' worth of work in my family." He ran a hand through his hair. "Oh that I still have time to rectify the problems of my father. And his before him, likely."

Jane looked away. "I'm sorry Algernon. I should have told you—"

The door opened with a knock, and a group of five heads peeked in.

Jane laughed. "Yes?"

"We're going to lunch, and we wondered if His Grace would like to join us."

Jane covered her smile.

Algernon was hungry, perhaps Jane would accompany them? He raised his eyebrows, but she shook her head. "You go ahead. I'm going to muddle through and create my altered thesis." She pointed at the ladies. "Bring me back a salad."

"Done." He stood, and two of the ladies immediately joined him at each arm. They were all smiles, and they led him from the room.

"Be careful with Algernon!" Jane's voice carried after them.

One of the women at his left muttered. "She worries too much. What could go wrong over lunch?"

"Nothing will go wrong! Where to, my fine new lady friends? I feel at a disadvantage. We have not yet been introduced . . ."

# CHAPTER 18

*J*ane shook her head. Algernon loved to have fun. Every now and then she caught a glimpse of that side of him, the side he said was always present in all his interactions before he jumped to her time. And she could tell he loved the ladies' attention. She knew her office staff was harmless, but what of this Anna? Was she from his time? She seemed so well acclimated, with wealth, a place in this society. It didn't seem likely she was secretly from Regency England, but one thing was certain, she knew more than she was saying.

Her phone dinged. And she laughed at the image. *Your friends are showing me how to take selfies.*

His head, surrounded by all the other ladies from the office who went, smiled back at her.

*You're already an expert! Well done.*

Then her phone rang. *Mother.* "Hello."

"Hello dear, just a quick reminder about dinner tonight. You said you would come as soon as you arrived. Your father is anxious to see you, and we all want to hear about your research in England."

Jane bit back her groan. She had forgotten. "Um, Mom, I have a friend here. From England. I don't know if we can make it."

"Bring your friend. She's always welcome. You know that."

"He might not feel comfortable."

The silence was filled with Jane's guesses as to her mother's expression.

"He is most definitely welcome also. Who is this friend?"

"Mom, just because he's a he doesn't mean there's anything more to know on the subject."

"But there is more to know. At least his name."

"Algernon Ramsbury."

She gasped. "That new duke from England?"

How on earth could her mother know that! "Mom, do you follow all the British tabloids?"

"Certainly not. His story was carried by plenty of respectable people, I'm sure."

"Okay, well, yes. So what time should be we there?"

"Seven, dear, and oh my, I better go buy extra."

"He's just like us, Mom."

"Of course he is dear. Do you think he likes American lasagna, or should I make something special?"

"Your lasagna is special. It's my favorite."

"Of course. Okay, I've got to go now." She hung up.

Oh boy. Jane had better prepare Algernon.

She dove back into her work and took advantage of the quiet office. As the hour crept on, she toyed with a modified thesis or two and had one question remaining.

Loud chatter from down the hall alerted everyone that lunch was over. Algernon shouted. "But we must do it at once!

Why are we returning when there is such a thing as carriage rides here in New York City?"

Jane shook her head and stuck it out of the office. "I'd think you'd be tired of such a thing."

"Jane." His face full of smiles, his voice speaking her name as a caress.

The other ladies gave her knowing looks and then separated into their cubicles.

"Hello, Algernon. So you had fun?"

"Delightful. My faith in America is restored. Your workmates are lovely people and so informative about you." He raised his eyebrows. "They told me all the hints and secrets about how to woo you and become your boyfriend."

"Algernon."

"What? Am I saying it incorrectly?"

"Yes, it loses its subtlety when spoken of in so blunt a manner. You might be best to stick with the Regency language you use so well."

He stepped closer. "You do react favorably when I suggest all manner of activities with a gentle, subtle flair." He waited until she returned his gaze. "I would be honored with your presence this evening."

"I'm happy to hear it, because my mother has invited us over for dinner." She closed one eye, squinting. "Sorry."

"No, this is tremendous. I would be equally honored to meet your parents." He entered the room and sat at one end of the table. "And now I have returned. They tell me that you will not wish to leave work early for a carriage ride, and so I am once again at your side, staring at these documents from the Lichfield family. Though I have been meaning to mention it, I cannot imagine what could be so fascinating about the inner workings of one family."

"You tell me. You seem to fall at the center of all their motivations." She opened up her book again to the page with the painting. "And I believe it has everything to do with that letter." She pointed to the crumbled paper in the lady's hand.

His phone rang. "Oh look at that! It works." He held it out. "How do I . . ."

Lady Anna's face smiled seductively at him, and Jane was tempted to ignore her call, but she showed him how to swipe to answer. "Now say hello."

"Hello, Lady Anna." His voice was overly loud.

"Shhh." Jane motioned for him to quiet.

He nodded. "I'm happy you called. We have questions for you about your family. Could you stop by?" He paused. "Yes, right now. Perfect. See you then."

Jane's mouth fell open. "What did you do?"

"I think the best way to find any of this information is to ask her yourself."

"I'm not sure she really has traveled through time."

"No better way to find out." His eyes held a challenge. She knew the reason she hesitated most was because of Lady Anna's hold over Algernon. She was afraid to lose him, though she knew he must leave some day, and believed he would likely never have come to America at all if she had given him the envelope from Nellie. Her guilt surged.

Within ten minutes, Lady Anna stood at the entry to their conference room. "Well, isn't this cozy?"

Jane stood. "Thank you for coming. Your input here could help us unravel all the remaining mystery."

"I don't know. I'll try to help."

"Algernon seems to think that you have a close relationship to these women, that you have firsthand knowledge?"

Lady Anna narrowed her eyes. "I'd prefer to leave my relationship vague." She sat and crossed her legs. "I do prefer the styles of our day to the drab Regency dresses, I'm sure you'll agree, Algie." Her dress fell open, leaving most of her leg bare.

He averted his eyes. "As of yet, I am more uncomfortable than anything else."

She laughed. "I imagine you could get used to it pretty quickly."

Jane cleared her throat. "Do you know which sister wrote this letter? It's signed, 'Lady Anna.'"

She waved her hand. "Then it was Lady Anna, of course. All the sisters wished for the duke's hand. She writes only what any of them would have. Never sent the letter, though. Shortly after they had other things to distract them, I'd imagine." She inspected her nails. "But what I wish to discuss is this lovely gala of yours. Everyone is coming, have you heard? All the big names here in New York, royals from Europe. Your Charles has created quite the stir. What did you offer him in exchange for all this assistance, I wonder?"

Jane reddened. "Nothing like what you're thinking, I'd imagine."

"Oh, come now, I am thinking nothing of the sort. You won't mind, of course, if I bid on Algie here, will you?"

"Of course. We could use all the donations we can get. I expect the Duke of Shelton to be the highest earner of the evening."

Algernon held up a finger. "Again, I'm reminded of Tattersalls. Must I be auctioned?" He winked, though, so Jane didn't worry too much about his whining.

She suspected he secretly enjoyed it and teased, "Do you suppose the women will faint dead away or just grapple with each other over who gets the highest bid?"

Anna raised her eyebrows. "Oh come now, Jane, let's not

pretend you aren't exactly accurate. He's in high demand, no matter the century."

Jane flipped the image. "Would you mind explaining just what his relationship was with this family?"

"I'm sure he can explain it himself." She pressed a finger into the table. "He offered himself to marry one of them, the highest bidder among them." She whispered. "That's why I find this auction so amusing, by the way." She cleared her throat. "The one of them who could offer the highest dowry would be married to the duke, and then he would help to find spouses for the rest of them."

Algernon stood up. His face blanched and then reddened. "Is that true?"

She narrowed her eyes. "Come now, no need to pretend you didn't know. Trying to impress Jane. I'm certain she's aware things like this happened all the time."

"They may have, but I was not involved. Anna, you know I had nothing to do with this plan."

Her eyes widened in disbelief. "Can you really not have known? They would say nothing to you? Your mother, your father not mention it?"

The incredulity on her face gave Jane pause. "How could you not know, Algernon?"

"You also would doubt me? There are many things my father did that I have no knowledge of. I have been avoiding all his correspondence and my steward and solicitor for many months now." He cleared his throat. "But I don't see how it's so harmful. One of the ladies marries into a duke's household, the rest into his family. Marriages for one and all. I don't see how it is too terribly awful. Many a woman would count them-selves blessed, and all of us good friends as well . . ."

"Well, for our family, it tore us apart, and your family did not do so well either, I'm sure you've discovered. All's well that ends well, so they say."

Jane shook her head. "But how are you here?"

"And this is where I stop disclosing any more information about my long lost ancestors." She leaned across Algernon so that her cleavage was clearly visible. "We are getting together tonight. Come."

Her voice, almost a purr, made Jane ill, but Algernon nodded as though entranced and said, "I'd love to."

"Wait. We have dinner with my parents." Jane blurted it out before she could stop herself, and Anna laughed.

"Oh, how quaint. Dinner with her parents. Do you know how that ends? Marriage. And you don't have time for such a thing."

Algernon's eyes apologized. "I forgot. Anna, let's catch up tomorrow night. Tonight is for Jane and her family."

Jane was one part embarrassed to have something as unglamorous as family dinner next to Lady Anna and all her plans and an equal part grateful. Algernon had class, twenty-first-century class as well as nineteenth century.

And then a deep familiar voice out in the hall filled her with dread. *Trent.*

"Um, she's in the conference room, Trent, but I don't think . . ." Chelsea's voice trailed off. And Trent filled the doorway. Algernon took a step back to give him room, which Trent took as a total admission of weakness. Jane shook her head as she noted the competitive gleam light his eye. But Lady Anna stepped forward. "Hello."

Jane could not believe the cross section of people standing in her conference room at that moment. Chelsea walked by and rolled her eyes.

"Trent. Hi. What are you doing here?"

He stepped in, nodded and winked at Anna, and draped his very heavy arm across Jane's shoulders. "I'm here to see my girlfriend."

Anna grinned. "Your girlfriend! Did you hear that, Algernon? Who knew our little Jane had a boyfriend?"

"He's not—"

"Certainly not I." A flash of hurt crossed Algernon's eyes.

Jane frowned. "Oh stop, everyone. Trent. Allow me to introduce Algernon and Anna. This is Trent, my *ex*-boyfriend."

"Come now, babe, we don't need to be adding ex's to things just yet. We've still got some junk to work through, but we can make it."

Anna tugged on Algernon's arm. "Perhaps we should leave so they can have a moment."

She started to pull him through the door, and Jane panicked. "No!"

Everyone turned to her after such an abrupt squeal.

"I, um, need to get going, that is, we—" She stepped up to Algernon and grabbed his other arm. "We need to be going to get ready for tonight."

Anna put a hand on her mouth, looking from Trent to Algernon and back. "If you're sure." She stepped closer to Trent. Jane could hear her words as they walked down the hall. "Now, who are you again?"

Jane let out a long breath. "That was awkward."

"I think I understand your context, and I completely agree."

"My parent's house is going to be a whole lot more so."

# CHAPTER 19

*T*hey had been sitting at the table for thirty minutes. Algernon enjoyed Jane's father, but he was unsure of her mother. She seemed so much like the matronly entrapping kind of mother that he held a great deal of suspicion about her motives for everything.

But her father talked sensibly, had a wonderful sense of humor, and asked him interesting questions, some of which he found difficult to answer.

"So, Algernon, what do you do for a living?"

"Well, I manage an estate in England and buy and sell horses."

Jane raised her eyebrows, obviously impressed with that spin on his completely useless lifestyle.

"Impressive. Where did you go to school? My Janie here is working on her dissertation." Her father's proud eyes made him grin, happy Jane came from a supportive home.

"I studied at Oxford, Eton before that, the usual over there."

Jane's father nodded. "I'm happy to hear my Jane has such a capable friend in you."

Did Algernon imagine it, or did her father emphasize the word *friend* just a little bit? He would be happy to further clarify his intentions toward the man's daughter, but he wasn't sure exactly what they were. Did he want to spend as much time as possible with her? Yes. Would he gladly kiss her senseless? Yes. Had he considered marrying her? His thoughts stuttered. Never before had he considered such a thing about any woman. But the answer came clearly and loudly into his brain. Yes. If it were in any way possible, he would consider marrying Jane. "I look forward to getting to know her better while I can."

"While you can?" Jane's mother's squeaky voice cut a path through his ear into his brain.

Jane put a hand on his arm. "Yes, Mother, Algernon has to get back to England, where he works, of course."

Her mother's dejected face would have amused Algernon if he didn't feel precisely the identical feelings her expression would indicate. "I regret that Jane is correct."

"Oh, that's too bad." Her mother's face was almost laughable, and Algernon recognized that mothers in any century had much in common.

Her father lifted his cup. "Your mother and I are looking forward to traveling."

"You are?" The incredulity in Jane's voice made him smile.

He cleared his throat. "Which we will do as soon as our Jane here is settled."

"Dad, you and Mom don't have to wait for me to get married before you have a life."

Algernon couldn't completely follow the logic in her parents' thinking, but he felt a twinge of sorrow for her situation, for it seemed they looked forward to handing her off, so to speak, before moving on in their lives.

They had finished up dinner, laughed, and enjoyed one

another's company until Algernon led Jane outside and into the car waiting to drive them. "I still don't quite understand how these cars just show up every time you need one."

Jane sidled up next to him, leaning against his arm as she held out her phone. "See, this square. You press it. It's for a car service. The nearest cars light up on your screen, and you can choose one to pick you up. Then when we are finished, we use the phone to pay him."

Algernon was fascinated. "We are so very far behind all of this where I am from. But of course you know that." He turned to face her before they got in the car. "I love that you know so much about where and when I'm from. I feel as though you are already a part of my home, even though I know that's impossible."

"I've always felt you were a part of mine."

He kissed the top of her head. "I don't know how we can possibly part. So often, I feel as though we are meant to be together." They climbed into the car.

Algernon's phone beeped. "Oh look! It's Anna, and she's got Trent with her."

"What! Are they on a date?"

"I can't tell. She says, *Come double with us.*" He turned to her. "Does she want us to go be with them as a couple together or separate?"

"That's the question of the hour."

"I'd rather be with you. Perhaps we can just have a night in?"

Jane was so pleased, she didn't try to stop her smile. "Excellent. I'll give the driver the address back to the apartment."

"Perhaps we can watch, what did you call it? A movie?"

"That sounds perfect, and you can tell me more stories from home."

"You never tire of those."

"It's true, I don't. But you should know, it's not really for my research that I love them so much. It is partially because I've always loved your time. But I also just want to hear your voice, learn about your life. Everything about you is fascinating to me."

Pleased, he pulled her up close beside him. "I enjoy these American customs of closeness. When I return I'm going to offend and ruin every woman if I keep this up."

"You'd best be on your guard."

"You are more correct than you realize." He snorted. "I would very much like for you to meet my mother."

"Oh? What's she like?"

"Forgive me and still think well of me, but she's terrible."

"What!" Jane's frown showed how unimpressed she was with his statement.

"I'm not even joking. She has had a rough go of it with my father, and she is a bundle of nerves and spiteful energy and is often wailing about something."

"Well, I bet a solid afternoon of love from her son and she might be on the mend before you know it."

Algernon doubted it, but he kept his further negative opinions to himself.

His phone dinged, and Jane groaned. "No, this is excellent!"

She sat up and leaned closer to see. "What?"

"My friend from the subway has responded to my correspondence. He wishes to meet up with us."

"You talk to him?"

"Well, certainly. I find him engaging and intelligent. Look, see." He scrolled through a long text message stream of Shakespeare quotes. "We share a common interest in classic literature."

Jane didn't know what to say. "Can we meet up with him later?"

He paused, his thumbs hovering over his phone, and Jane couldn't shake the strangeness of the image. Then he nodded. "Quite right. You and I have a previous engagement at home." He typed something, then he pulled her closer to him again. "That sounds so nice, at home."

They at last arrived at the apartment building and waited for the elevator to take them up to the twenty-seventh floor. "I try to become accustomed to the idea of some things, like you living so high up in the sky, but I cannot. I see it, but it remains unfathomable to me."

"I guess it would." She opened the door, and they entered.

The space felt suddenly very small and Jane very close. "Perhaps we could play music and dance?"

Jane smiled, "Wonderful idea. But I don't have your dance music; perhaps I'll show you what we do here?"

"I have a feeling I may like that way too much."

"We'll be all right." She moved to the black box that sat on shelves and pushed some buttons and then did something on her phone.

He pulled out his phone. "I'm going to miss my phone when I have to go back."

"You'll forget all about it soon enough."

The music started. It sounded strange to his ears, but nice, slow, a steady beat. He pulled her into his arms as Anna had done with him at the club. But he wiped away her superficial and imbibed image and just enjoyed the feel of Jane.

She wrapped her arms around his back and leaned her head on his chest. "This is how we do things here."

"I like this." They swayed together, his hands running up and down her back, playing with her hair, letting its silky strands fall between his fingers. "But the dances of our day have a purpose."

"They do. You're correct, and I love to dance them."

"But tonight, this is just right." He guided them around the room, following the beat and the slow swaying motion, almost as if they were waltzing.

"Of course you dance even our modern dances better than anyone I know."

He rested his chin on her head. "I shall remember you just like this for many years to come."

She sighed. "I can't let you go." Her tiny voice ended in a hiccupping sigh.

"Are you crying?" He pulled away to see the tears. And his heart ached for her. "Allow me to lessen your pain."

She didn't respond, burying her head in his chest.

"I would do anything if I could erase this sense of duty I feel to my estate. I must correct the wrongs I have enabled for too long. I am filled with questions, what ifs. I must return to see if the estate can yet be saved."

"I understand. I'm so selfish. You'll soon see how selfish I am and then hate me. I'm just not ready for you to leave."

"One half of the man inside me wants to never leave your side, but the other half is plagued by guilt and responsibility. And that half clamors the loudest. Would that I could understand how to return home and get there sooner."

She looked away.

"I don't mean I wish for our time to be shortened, but I am encumbered with the weight of my title as if the whole line of my ancestors were calling down to me mandating that I do my duty."

"The gala is next week."

"Ah yes, my time in Tattersalls." He smirked. "You know I'm

happy to help you. I feel that when I do leave, you will be in the best possible way. Your work saved, your research unique and accurate. I'm quite proud of you, you know."

"I could have done nothing without you. It was because of you I could even look at the research, because of you that I understand some of it."

"Fate is just such a kind creature sometimes. Because she brought me you, someone I never would have met otherwise, in my time or yours. The very idea that we could be together is almost laughable, and yet, here we are." He pulled her closer, but she stiffened.

"Laughable?" Her face fell. "Because I'm a commoner." She turned away. "You do find me beneath you." She stepped back. "And you are counting the days until you can leave."

He tried to pull her back close again, but she wouldn't come. "I find no lasting value to the term *commoner*, just pointing out that something as drastic as our current circumstances had to happen in order for us to meet."

She shrugged, her face pained. "Perhaps we should go to bed."

"If that's what you want. But be reasonable, it's not just our class that stands between us otherwise. I was born over two hundred years ago . . ."

She turned from him and made her way to her back bedroom. As she got to the door, she turned, and Algernon filled with hope.

"I've never been enough for you, not from the moment you saw me, not even now. You will always see me as common."

"It doesn't matter to me. I can't pretend it's not true, but it has no bearing on my feelings."

"You've always been outside my reach, then, a picture in a

book, and now, standing right here in front of me." She turned from him and shut the door behind her.

And Algernon allowed his frustration to rise. What more could he say to the woman? She was choosing not to listen or believe him. Perhaps it was for the best they had an emotional distance since he was leaving her anyway. The sooner the better. He just had to figure out how he could possibly return to his time. A return to England, of course, was necessary. And Anna could manage that. He was certain another talk with that woman, Nellie, would also be required. He had some questions for her before he went back, or rather, he could ask her during his time as well. She had been in both places. He couldn't fathom how that was possible. The other person he wanted answers from was Anna. He suspected her to be the same girl he played with as a child, but he didn't believe for one minute that they had all been pining away for a proposal from him. Each one of them had refused to be dependent on marriage. They'd been irritated by the thought since he was little, even knowing the reality as they did, the reality that their very livelihood depended upon a marriage to a man, or at least finding one who would take care of them.

Anna texted just then. *I want to talk. And we're still out enjoying New York. Come play. Bring Jane if you must. Better see as much as you can before you go back next week.*

*Next week? How do you know when I'm going back?*

*The full moon . . . just come. We're waiting outside your building.*

*Okay, I'll be right there.*

He sent a text to Jane, and waited to see if she would come. But after a minute, when she didn't answer, he left without her. Anna was right. He wanted to see New York, wanted to enjoy his time before he had to go back. If Jane refused to do so with him, then he'd go out with Anna and Trent and whoever else.

He grimaced when he thought of how enormous that man was. Surely muscles so enlarged were unnatural.

He opened the outside door to a happy Anna who walked at his side, her arm around him at the waist. "Let's go have some fun, Your Grace."

"I'm in the mood for fun." He stopped, squinting to see who else was in the car. "That's not . . ."

"It is, but he's sorry. See." She opened the door.

The baron held up his hands. "I'm totally and completely sorry, Your Grace. Come on."

Charles reluctantly sat beside the baron, and the others who were in town for the auction joined them as well. Some people he recognized from the house party. "What are we waiting for? Let's go!"

They cheered when he got in, and Anna joined them. Four other girls who he'd never seen were a part of the group. They paired off with each of the men, so he supposed he was to be with Anna. As long as she didn't try anything like last time, he supposed there was only fun to be had. "Charles, you've gathered quite a group."

Lord Smithy grunted. "Yes, Charles was very persuasive."

"I've good motivation. That research she's seen is valuable."

Algernon nodded. "I'd imagine it is. Who'd have thought that a time period so long ago could be so fascinating to so many now?"

Anna snorted. "I've said the same thing a time or two."

She understood him. He draped an arm across her back, enjoying the familiarity, and cheered when they suggested dancing. All this responsibility, the guilt, the plans for the future were beginning to weigh on him. It was time to rebirth his more reckless nature and behave in a manner entirely uncouth.

# CHAPTER 20

$\mathcal{T}$he next week was filled with intense work on Jane's paper, rushed breakfasts with Algernon, and his consistent absence in the evening hours. On the far side of that week, Jane stood at the head of a large ballroom, ready for the gala to begin. The décor was extravagant, the dinner prepared, the tables ready. The invitations sent and replies received. Everything was in readiness—except for the men in breeches. *Where was Algernon?*

They were on good terms, if a bit platonic for her liking. He was nothing if not respectful. Breakfast stories were the most amusing part of her day. He'd taken to spending time with a biker gang, the man from the subway. They were surprisingly literate, well read. Apparently Algernon spent time discussing Shakespeare. All she could do was shrug and think, *Who knew?*

She had resisted the urge to text him early this morning when the couch was empty, obviously not slept in. If he was going to sleep away, that was his business. She had taken out her phone and then stopped her fingers and put the phone back in her purse numerous times all morning, refusing to go begging, but now she was almost in a panic. Not one of her participants had arrived yet, and the gala would begin in forty-five minutes.

Her thumbs flew over the letters. She could reach out to Charles. He was the one who had gathered the others. *Getting nervous. Where are you?*

Three dots for a reply, she held her breath. *On our way. I thought Algie had explained. Had a bit of a night, but we are ready and handsome as ever . . . in breeches.* His eye-rolling emoji would have made her laugh on any other day.

*So, expected time of arrival?*

*Five minutes.*

She let her air out in one steady stream. They were coming. And all put together? Last night she'd ignored yet another of Algernon's texts inviting her to come but had listened for the door to close. Upon hearing it, she went into the kitchen for a drink of water. She couldn't bear another night out with him and the others, the only commoner in the bunch. And besides, she felt guilty. After listening to him talk about how desperately he wished to return, she realized how much his past, his present, whatever, had been weighing on him, how much he longed to save his estate. Of course he would. She should have given him the letter from Nellie. She would have last night. But then she'd let her hurt show, actual tears, and she'd been mortified. And then he'd seemed so caught up in his life back home he didn't appear as if he would miss her at all, which sat wrong. She was selfish. She knew it, but she was in love with a man who was bent on leaving her forever and didn't seem to mind. The hurt tore at her heart. She didn't know how she would survive without him. But tonight she would give him the envelope from Nellie. He would be furious. She knew it, and that was okay, because then he would leave her forever.

And she could return to staring at his image in the portrait. And watching for history to change. Perhaps he could do something important and save his estate after all.

The AV guy finished doing a sound check for the room. Jane felt fidgety. Then the back door opened. Algernon entered, and her mouth went dry. He wore a leather jacket on top of his Regency clothing. And he wore it well. His eyes sparkled in humor. He turned in a circle and slipped the jacket off.

"I see the jacket had the correct effect. I look hot, do you think?" His grin, full of the wicked and the delicious, warmed her to her toes.

"Yes, you look hot in the jacket. Save it for later." Her wink made him pause at her front, his eyes going dark.

"Most definitely."

She eyed him and went through a mental checklist. Full ballroom attire, breeches, jacket, cravat, crisp and to perfection; his hair, just right; tall, black shiny hessians, all dressing the best man of her acquaintance, who stood mere inches away. She resisted the urge to fall into his arms, but only just. It helped to remember he had been out all night with no explanation and Lady Anna was involved.

Behind him were Charles and a team of ten men who had no business being in one place looking so handsome.

And then Lady Anna. Her face, confident, all knowing, a slight smirky rise to one corner of her mouth. And Jane wanted to order her from the room. But that was unfair, and the woman would probably bid on Algernon. They needed her pocketbook.

So Jane pasted on a smile and explained the instructions to the group. "I wanted to thank you again for doing this. Our society will be saved because of your generosity."

Charles cleared his throat.

"Yes, and a special thanks to Charles for gathering everyone and helping them arrive on time." She knew he was expecting help with his research, and Jane would pay him back.

As soon as she got the signal from the back, they would be opening the doors. She shooed the men to their dressing room and told Anna where she was to be seated.

Light music began in the background, the doors opened, and the room began to fill with beautiful people in gorgeous clothing. And Jane felt her excitement rise. People were coming! It would be a success. On entrance tickets alone, they were almost to their goal. The bidding would put them over the top, needed funds if they were to expand and improve their library or increase in the line of research her dissertation would begin.

Their hired emcee took the mic, and dinner began. Her phone dinged. Algernon. *Sorry we were late.*

*I was almost in a panic.*

*I forgot I could text you. The others said I was an idiot.*

*Not an idiot. But thank you.* She bit her lip, unsure she wanted to even know. *How was your evening?*

*I learned a new word: epic.*

Her heart sank.

*But would have been better with you.*

She sent him heart emojis. She wondered if he even knew about emojis. Everything about Algernon still felt so surreal to her.

*I invited a few extra guests, I hope you don't mind . . .*

*How many?*

*They should be arriving soon.* He sent back a thumbs up. Impressive. Her Regency man had mastered modern texting habits. She had ruined him forever for his time. She laughed.

The others at her table glanced at her in question. He would return to a time when a missive to a lady was paramount to a proposal of marriage. Two hundred years had certainly changed courting habits. Another fantastic research topic.

The doors opened again to another set of broad-shouldered gentlemen, and she couldn't quite place them. The first approached, and he handed her his card. *Band of Brothers.*

She gasped. The man from the subway. *Wow, he cleaned up nice.* She told the staff to set another table at the back, which they did, immediately. "Welcome. They are just getting your table ready now."

He nodded his head and then jerked for the others to follow. They looked amazing in suits, bow ties, the occasional chain hanging out of a pocket.

Soon everyone was seated, eating, and happy. At last they cleared dinner, and the time for the auction had everyone buzzing with loud chatter, women sitting on the edge of their seats, and the men laughing.

One by one her contestants came out, posing as if they belonged in *GQ*. Women squealed, screamed, and cheered . . . and bid. And the numbers rose higher and higher. Close-up shots of their faces filled screens behind them as each paraded across the front.

The guests received a program with a bio and headshot of each participant. She glanced through each of them, mostly checking for typos in a maniacal desire to ensure perfection even though at this point there was nothing she could do about a single mistake she might find. Algernon's was blank but for one line. He had submitted only, "Her Regency man."

Jane's heart went up in her throat. She tried to swallow it down, but tears sprang to her eyes. She did not deserve him. Gifted these few weeks with the most important man to ever enter her life, and she had spent most of the time fixated on research, her life's work. But in reality all her theories and suppositions were interesting, but everything she studied was his actual life, which she neglected to really recognize. She had hid details from him about how to return home and had selfishly tried to keep him only for herself. She would tell him tonight. Even though she knew the information would dim the appreciative light that always lit his face when he looked at her. He deserved to go and to leave when he chose, not when she finally revealed how. She assumed the letter held that information. Nellie had alluded to as much.

And then Algernon walked out on the stage. And there was a collective gasp. He was magnificent. A power emanated from him she had never noticed before. He carried himself like she imagined a duke would. He seemed certain of a knowledge of his importance in the world, his worth. And for the first time she didn't notice any sense of better-ness, just a strong understanding of his place. Perhaps she had misunderstood. Perhaps the only difference between them was this strong sense of self she lacked.

Perhaps she had imagined his belittling nature, perhaps he had never viewed her as truly common. She shook her head at her own insecurities and then, almost without thinking, raised her hand to bid one thousand dollars.

Algernon turned to her, his eyebrow raised.

Of course Anna countered and raised the bid to five thousand dollars, which she could not counter, but as he paraded in front of her table, he winked. The bidding rose, higher and higher, the highest yet. Someone shouted, "Fifteen thousand pounds." The room hushed. That was nearly—

The auctioneer called out, "By way of information, that is the equivalent of $19,650. Do I hear twenty thousand?"

"Twenty-five thousand." Lady Anna's face was determined.

An elderly lady in the back raised her hand. "Thirty thousand."

And to Jane's disbelief it continued. Chelsea approached at her right. "The woman in the back is a matron from England. It is rumored she is a relation of Algernon's."

She was small, but elegant. She raised her hand again. "Fifty thousand dollars."

A hush followed. The auctioneer called it again and again, and then, "Sold! For fifty thousand dollars."

Algernon bowed to the woman and then smiled as he came to sit beside Jane. "That's incredible, isn't it?"

She nodded, breathless. "It is."

The emcee nodded at her, and she jumped up. "I forgot."

Algernon squeezed her hand, and she clung to that moment of pressure on her fingertips as the lifeline she needed to do what she must, to lose him. She wasn't sure she could ever be the same again now that she'd had him in her life, even for a time as brief as these few weeks had been.

She stood in front of the mic, opened the envelope Chelsea had given her, and felt tears fill her eyes again. She swallowed, struggling to find words. She looked to Algernon for strength. The amount raised was overwhelming. It was such a gift. She nodded at Charles. Algernon came to stand beside her, his presence anchoring her to the task. "I am overwhelmed. My great thanks to all who made this possible. I wish you all the best on your dates this evening. As a group, we have earned two hundred fifty thousand dollars for our historical society."

The crowd stood and cheered. "And we will use this money to continue research about a time that fascinates us all, about the women during that time who are so underestimated by some, and to continue our tribute to authors from that time, namely and especially Jane Austen herself." She bowed. "My many thanks again."

And then it was finished. People mingled and gathered, the men in breeches finding their winning bidders. Jane watched them for a moment.

"You are pleased." Algernon's deep voice in her ear rose goosebumps on her arms.

"Gooseflesh." He ran a hand over her skin, which only increased their presence and sent shivers through her, trembling ripples. "Are you cold? Or . . ."

"Not cold." She turned to him, not bothering to hide her desire. "Algernon, I—"

"There you are, my boy, come to me, my dear." The winning bidder for Algernon.

With a large amount of regret in his expression, he then turned to her with a smile and a bow. "With great pleasure, my lady. I am yours for the evening."

She laughed and tapped his arm with her fan. "You shouldn't say such things nowadays. People will completely misunderstand your intentions."

Jane's eyes sharpened, and she and Algernon shared a glance, but his date widened her eyes innocently enough and said nothing more.

Algernon bowed to Jane. "I'll see you later."

"Yes."

"Oh, dear me. Just a moment. I must speak with someone. Do be a dear and wait for me here?" She patted his arm and walked across the room.

Jane stepped closer. "There's something I must tell you. It is urgent."

But Lady Anna approached. "It's for the best I didn't win, I suppose. You're going home during the full moon, are you not?"

"What has the full moon to do with it?"

Anna turned to Jane who cleared her throat.

"Surely Jane told you. Nellie left her with specific instructions."

Algernon's eyes widened. "Jane?"

"Well, I—"

Anna's eyes narrowed. "Yes, she told me herself that all the information had been passed along. You can return at any full moon, but you must do so at Twickenham."

"I was not aware, no." His deep eyes seemed to search her soul. "You knew this? And didn't tell me?" His eyes clouded, and at once he seemed distant. Then he nodded his head at Jane and Anna and moved to greet his approaching date for the evening.

"I don't blame you, you know." Anna stood beside her, watching him escort the effusively talking woman. "He is quite irresistible."

"Oh stop. I feel as terrible as I've ever felt. I've ruined everything."

"You've ruined nothing. I wouldn't allow you to do something so drastic. He'll be home in plenty of time to save the estate, his and mine. All's well that ends well, don't they say?"

Jane looked away.

"Oh, but you were talking about ruining something else, weren't you?" She hummed. "Yes, well, that might be the case. And it might not. I went to visit a few old friends and learned some important details about you. I've underestimated you. You might have what it takes to snag our big Algie. Only time"—she winked—"will tell."

She swung her hips as she left Jane.

Even though Jane had saved the society, created an incredible thesis with a bold and new thesis statement backed by irrevocable evidence, she felt empty and cold and wanted nothing more than to see Algernon's smile of approval instead of the lifeless look of utter disappointment he had left her with.

# CHAPTER 21

*A*lgernon checked his phone for the tenth time while the driver loaded his trunks into the limo. He was bringing back an additional trunk full of items he now could not live without. Shaving powder, being one, deodorant, gym shorts. Socks. And toothbrushes were lovely. The paste felt a bit powerful on his tongue, burned, but he soon accustomed, and he knew he would miss the fresh feeling. Images. He had printed as many as he could find of Jane.

His heart dropped again. How dreadful to fall in love with a woman as selfish as she. Had she ever loved him? Or merely used him for her own benefit? He tried to shake her from his mind, but she persisted in an unrelenting agony as he knew she would for many months yet.

Well, such was his lot. He didn't expect to be overly happy for the foreseeable future, learning how one's father had destroyed the family name, how he was blamed for not doing his part, rescuing one's estate, dinner parties, and his mother. No, he didn't see much to be enjoyed in the near future, but perhaps, after a time, he could find happiness again.

And now that he knew the secrets of time travel, he could return, if only to stock up on supplies.

Lady Anna had been most helpful. He would be using her private jet. She didn't return with him. Apparently she and Trent, the overly large muscular ex-boyfriend of Jane's, had a date tonight. Algernon shook his head. He had never pictured Anna as the marrying type. He was nearly certain she was the same Anna of his childhood. She chose to leave any questions pressing her for particulars unanswered. He shrugged. What did it matter? He had no desire for a close relationship with her. He hesitated. Rather, he might if it would save his estate. The letters of Jane's seemed to indicate conversations had at one point been initiated but had ceased. Perhaps when the girls traveled through time. He didn't blame them. Regency England was a far cry from 2019 for women.

Without too much trouble, he and his trunks were loaded onto the plane. He recognized what Anna had been trying to explain to him. Nobles did exist in 2019, whether titled or not, and their lives were enhanced by privilege, bought with an excess of money. And their lifestyle seemed significantly easier, just as it was during his time. The fact that Jane didn't share this ease never bothered him. It was so freeing, during 2019, to not feel the constraint of class and title.

Another reason to return to visit. He winced. Would it hurt so terribly every time? This time? The pain in his head and around his eyes. The full moon began in one day, twelve hours after he landed in Heathrow airport.

The worst part about going home? Not being able to tell a single soul about his experiences. No one would believe him, and Bedlam was a looming risk for some.

He closed all the window shades firmly and told the pilot he was free to take off.

Then he leaned his chair back and tried to forget that the vibrations and the noise meant he was leaving the earth to hang precariously in the sky, over a vast ocean. Even more difficult, he tried to forget that when he left New York, he was leaving Jane forever. They hadn't said goodbye. He couldn't bear to see her again. The sooner he put her behind him, the less he would be continually hurt by her memory, by her lack of caring.

She had left the envelope with his time travel instructions on his things. Written across the front, in small letters only, *I'm sorry.*

Arriving at Twickenham was surprisingly easy, too easy, and before he knew it, before he was prepared, he was once again standing in front of Nellie.

"You have quite an amazing system going on here."

She nodded. "We do."

"I can return again?"

"You can, right now, on a full moon."

"So, is it the same 'you' here who is in all the times? When I see you in my time, will you also be here?"

One of the maids made a clucking noise in the corner.

"Don't try to think of it in that way. Your mind will not be able to grasp our magic."

He didn't want to discuss it further with her. He just wanted to go home. "Will it hurt like last time?"

She nodded. "Probably. Magic always has a price. It might be worse when we do it without a painting."

Nellie raised a hand over his head, and the glowing powder showered down around him. The tingles, then the sharp stabs of pain, then the dizzy spell. When he opened his eyes, he lay on the floor alone, in the same room, but it was dank and cold. He had forgotten how nice central heating could be, and as he had hoped, his trunks had traveled with him.

He stood. A maid entered. "Oh, Your Grace!"

"Yes, it is I." He brushed off his clothing. "If you could call for my carriage and alert my valet, it is time to return home." He wobbled on his feet. Nothing hurt nearly as badly this time.

"But you've only just arrived!"

His smile started small and then grew. "It's as if I never left."

She curtsied, but as she turned to go, he thought he saw a glimmer about her, a spark of something. Perhaps she was in on the magic too.

The journey home was laborious. But he at last arrived and headed straight for his father's study. He rang the servant bell pull. When a sleepy maid answered, he called for some tea and for a note to be sent to his steward to meet as soon as he was able.

Then he pulled down his father's books, wiped dust from the cover, took a deep breath in preparation, and opened the first page.

JANE WOKE TO A DREARY, overcast, rain-filled day. She pulled a pillow over her head and for a moment refused to leave her bed. She had folded up the blanket on the couch, but she hadn't washed the pillow case, instead burying her face in it, hoping the smell of her Regency man would bring him back.

How terribly and incredibly wrong she had been about him the whole time. What could be worse than to come to the realization that an amazing man had left her life? Forever. He had not seen her as common, not at all. Obviously. She pulled the pillow tighter over her face and screamed into its softness. She was so consistently and stupidly blind. Instead of being appalled at her presence, he had lived with her, done her bidding, supported her fundraiser, and aided in her research. How could a person be as completely deluded as she? Insecurity had ruled the day. And selfishness.

The buzzer rang. It rang again. Someone downstairs was trying to reach her.

She wrapped a robe around herself and made her way to the intercom. She pressed the button down with her thumb. "Yes?"

"We have a package here for Jane Sullivan. From England."

"Bring it up."

She padded to the kitchen, pouring orange juice in a cup. Evidence of Algernon was everywhere. Even though he hadn't slept over the night before, her cups were misplaced. Every item he had used was in a different place than she would have put it. Again she was touched he had tried to clean up. Never once in his entire ducal life had he been required to clean up after a meal. She was certain of it. Her heart warmed toward him further and pined for him more. She doubted she would ever meet anyone like him.

And she had ruined his trust.

And he was gone forever. She chided herself. She was going to have to let this go. She knew he would leave. That was no surprise. But they had left at the worst possible moment in their relationship. Knowing that he was alive in his time, at his estate, thinking horribly of her, made life unbearable. The words of Jane Austen sounded in her brain, and never before had she felt such a kinship to Elisabeth Bennet. *I cannot bear to think he is alive in the world and thinking ill of me.* Knowing that technically he had already died in her time made her ill. That he went to his grave thinking ill of her. She wanted to climb back into bed.

But the knock on the door brought her into the living room.

A courier held an oversized package. "Sign here."

From Lady Anna.

The door closed, and she stared. The box was the typical size of a portrait. Her palms felt clammy as she clumsily searched through her junk drawer for the scissors.

With all the cardboard peeled back, she tore off the padding and choked out a sob. Her painting. The woman, clutching a note. Jane's gaze whipped to the corner. Algernon smiled in the corner, but now, his smile was different. She stared, mesmerized. He was no longer smirking, hiding a secret, now he was openly grinning, as if he'd just received excellent news. His eyes sparkled with caring. As she analyzed it more, she recognized the mystery there. He still asked a question. And his eyes. The artist had captured their warmth. Could he still feel kindly toward her? Surely he knew she would see his image.

How could this be? It was all too vast for her mind to grasp.

She carried it into her office. Anna had sent no other note or message, just, the painting.

While she waited for her desktop computer to turn on, she studied anything else she might find familiar. Everything looked the same, except for his one expression. She snorted. Well, at least he wasn't miserable at home. She huffed. Not that she wanted him to be, but he never did seem to be as bothered as she was about their separation.

Finally she pulled up the search engine and typed in his name.

All the latest news of the past month scrolled through first.

*Famous duke is finally found. Last remaining member of the Ramsbury family.* Then another one. *Duke of Shelton finds doppelganger.*

That's new! She opened it and read an article about a current duke of Shelton, alive now, shaking hands with Algernon. Incredible. So that meant . . . She clicked a few more links.

Image after image of the Shelton estate. The Shelton foundation. The Shelton school of the arts. Amazed, she couldn't believe everything she was seeing. He'd done it. She sat back, great feelings of pride filling her, pride she had no right feeling. He'd saved his estate. She pulled up more reputable sites. Now she wanted to read the history. She wanted to read everything about him.

Her email dinged.

Lady Anna. *You'll want to read these. You're welcome.*

Links, twenty links to all the information about Algernon. She emailed back. *Thank you, and for the painting. He seems happy.*

She didn't respond. Anna only responded when she wanted to; Jane already knew that.

Jane texted Chelsea. *Not coming in. I'll explain later.*

Then she pulled up the first link. And the next, and many hours later, the final link. He'd done it. Almost. And he was one of the most remarkable men of his time. Tears streamed down her face. "Well done, Algernon." But as she continued to read, she discovered he never quite restored his estate in his lifetime, just preserved it. He'd had to sell off most of his holdings. His title became more of a courtesy title over the years, through the generations, in recognition of all he'd tried to do, but in reality, the estate was all but gone.

And that made her very sad. Maybe there was something to

be done. Lady Anna. She seemed to have access to both worlds, had been there, perhaps?

Jane padded back to the kitchen. When she opened the fridge she nearly screamed in surprise. Algernon's face was on the maple syrup bottle. She took it out with shaking hands. *Algie Syrup*. What on earth. The tiny italics blurb said, *Thanks to Algie Syrup, England's oldest and tastiest maple syrup.*

She shook her head. "You are something."

After a refill of her orange juice, she opened up her laptop, moved to the couch in the living room, and began to type. Somehow, Algernon's actions from two hundred years ago inspired her to do something just as meaningful today.

One link had concerned her, something to do with the Lichfield estate. She opened it up. She knew from her research most of the sisters had all but disappeared from history. One small line in the family remained, which would explain Lady Anna's presence in 2019. Many thought them spinsters. And some suspected it had to do with a sibling spat over Ramsbury, but she knew that wasn't true. The longer she researched, the more she realized that what truly must have happened was a new fascination with time travel. Since Anna seemed to know all about its existence and to know all about who Ramsbury was, she was either one of the sisters, turned modern, or a descendant of some kind.

How were the Ramsbury and Lichfield estates linked? Why did one matter to the other?

She pulled up her research and started to study the files. Something was right in front of her, something she'd missed.

Images and links about Ramsbury kept coming up in her search for the Lichfield sisters. And the more she read, the more she wished there was something she could do for them. For Ramsbury. He needed money to save his estate. It seemed, after he left her, all his efforts to gain more money had kept him afloat; he helped many people, had apparently revolutionized the maple syrup industry in London, but none of it came to fruition much in his lifetime. And the research was incredibly silent on the subject of marriage. She didn't know what to think about that. Was she relieved or happy not to have to see a happy marriage for him? Saddened. She was sad. All of it made her sad. He deserved more.

So, he needed money. She clicked more, opening up her resources from the library system, studied the Lichfields and their situation. They seemed to be under the same sort of problem. They showed little interest in marrying and had no entail on their estate, and yet their resources were limited, or at least they behaved as though they were.

But why would Ramsbury's father have sought them as a possible marriage for his son, with the hopes to bring in more money to save the estate if they didn't appear to be very wealthy? What was she missing?

She dug through her research from their house, amassed from all the hours of time, looking for the tiniest hint.

The letters about marrying Ramsbury seemed to allude to the possibility of more wealth were he to do so. But where was this wealth to come from?

# CHAPTER 22

*A*lgernon Ramsbury, the Duke of Shelton, stood at the entryway of Almack's, trying desperately not to be bored. To no avail. What he wanted was one of those hot dogs on the corner of Fifth and Broadway. His friends had deserted him, opting to sit at the tables tonight, but he had sworn off all games of chance. His finances were in such a state that he'd sworn off anything extravagant for the foreseeable future. But he had plenty of hope and lists and lists of ideas to help increase his income. His steward and he had worked long into the night every evening this week. The man was a veritable fiend—in a helpful way—when it came to setting an estate in order, taking great joy in anything relating to numbers and finances. He was as excited as Algernon at all the possibilities of bringing in more wealth.

In truth, Algernon was excited about all possibilities but one. The purpose for his attendance at this ball. To secure a wife, a wealthy one.

He couldn't abide the thought. His father had, in fact, tried to secure a match with the Lichfield family, but as Algernon had suspected, correspondence with the family had stalled, and according to rumor, they hadn't been seen in public for many years.

His gaze traveled through the room. Many of the ladies were remarkably attractive. He should be enjoying himself, knowing they all would be happy to rest their hands on his arms, to dance with him, to marry him. He had his pick of the whole season. But he was dissatisfied. And he knew why, but he couldn't bring himself to admit he missed Jane. Or even any American woman, to be honest, but particularly Jane.

And every blasted female present wore gloves.

Something new surprised him. Along the wall, a number of artists painted, watching the evening play out to their front. An ache in his heart reminded him of the painting that Jane had so loved. So this was how such a work had come to be. A new trend, perhaps?

And then Lady Anna stepped into the room. He looked twice before he realized it wasn't her from just one week past, but most certainly the Anna from his childhood. Interesting. They were not one and the same as he'd sometimes suspected. But surely this Anna and the Anna in Jane's time had met somehow, the other knew too much. He watched her search the room until he stepped forward, and then her face broke out into a large smile. She hurried to him. "I knew I would find you here."

"It's the biggest party of the season so far. I'm surprised to see you, though. It's been years, and we haven't heard a word from your family."

"No, no, I *knew* I would find you here. Tonight's the night, isn't it?"

He tilted his head. "What are you saying?"

She indicated the painters along the wall. "They're here, I'm here, you're here, and I made sure to bring this." She pulled a paper out of her dress.

Algernon was beginning to understand. "The painting? Jane's?"

She nodded. "I think so; all I know is I'm supposed to be here, tonight, with you." She handed him the letter. "And you're to read this."

*Dear Algie,*

*As you are right now probably starting to guess, this is the moment where the painting is created that Jane looks at all these years. Smile pretty. People will be studying your face for over two hundred years.*

*Anna*

He searched Lady Anna's face. "Would you care to dance?"

She watched him but did not seem to have any more information to offer. "No, I can't, you must stand in the corner."

"But to what purpose? What do you know?"

Her eyes widened, "to keep history repeating itself. We have estates to save, don't we?"

"We? Are you saving your estate as well?"

"We need Jane, so no matter what has happened between you, just go smile so things can move forward like they should."

A man approached and asked Lady Anna to dance. She looked meaningfully at Algernon, indicating he should stand in the corner.

But he didn't want to stand in the corner. His heart ached. And he wanted to understand. And he didn't want to go smirk for Jane's picture. *Her Regency man.* He balked at the idea. She had betrayed him, selfishly withheld knowledge. He shook his head; how could she? He would never forgive her for that. He had thought himself done with her, that all he now needed to do was allow the healing passage of time. But here he was, re-creating the moment that would enable her own fascination with him. But perhaps it was more than that, perhaps it was a moment for historians in their time, like Lady Anna said.

He leaned against the wall in the corner, his gaze traveling over the room. He thought of Jane and wondered, what good would it do to harbor such negative feelings for someone he would never see again?

And truth be told, he would give anything to see her again. He hated leaving things the way he had. Even if she had betrayed him, he wished he'd made some kind of amends with her before he left. Knowing he would be dead two hundred years before she would even think of him again made him ill. He longed for one more moment. But he knew such a thing was impossible. Even if he went back, he planned to avoid her. What good would it do to keep feelings burning that were better off dying? The best thing would have been a responsible conversation before he left.

What did this painting have to do with saving the Lichfield estate, or his own, for that matter? He thought through what it must have felt like on her end, remembered all the times she'd wished he could stay. He felt eyes on him. Artists were staring, taking his likeness. And suddenly a realization crashed around him with the force of a jolt forward on the New York subway. She delayed telling him because she loved him. She didn't want him to leave. And that seemed like a good enough reason to be selfish. And of a sudden, he could forgive her. He didn't care that she delayed his return. What did it matter? He could choose the time of his return and no one was any wiser. Knowing she was looking, two hundred years from now, he suddenly felt all the anger fizzle away, leaving only his gratitude and love—yes, love—for Jane Sullivan. His face broke out into a smile. She loved him. And he loved her back. He grinned, imagining he saw her again, knowing she would open the page of her book to stare at him, knowing again that fate had brought them together, and he couldn't help but smile. And as soon as he imagined seeing Jane again, his smile grew. He couldn't stop if he tried. Instead, he tried to show reconciliation, to show what he should have said before he left. He smiled all his love to her. It was the only thing he could do, and he hoped that she would understand.

As soon as the dance was over, Lady Anna joined him in his corner.

"Now, would you care to dance?"

"Going to try and court me, Your Grace?"

"Would that be so difficult to believe? I heard my father was inclined to pursue the idea."

"When he thought we had money."

"Come now, that sounds so crass."

"But that's what you're after, aren't you? Be honest. We played as children. We all know how the game works. You can stop right now. I'll save you the effort. Your father was deluded, grasping for straws. There is no wealth. We all have but a few thousand to our names for dowries."

"But why would he think there was? Look, Lady Anna. I'm speaking now as a friend. I have no interest in combining our estates."

Her face looked troubled, the rose of her cheeks warming prettily. Ramsbury vowed to help her find a good match.

She waved her hand around. "There are rumors, ridiculous

speculations about ancient money, but there is none. Believe me, if there was, we sisters would know about it."

Intrigued, he kept her hand on his arm when the music ended and led her to a corner. "What are we talking about here? A hidden treasure?"

She shrugged. "There is no substance to the rumors. We looked as children, searched every cave."

He snorted. "I imagine you would have, and I as well, had I known. How intriguing. My estate has nothing so exciting rumored about it, just its eventual ruin."

Her eyes widened in sympathy. "How bad is it?"

"I think I can prevent its ruin, but it will never flourish as it once did." His resentment toward his father resurfaced. "Blast the incredible irresponsibility of the men in my family."

She raised an eyebrow.

"And I would have been just as negligent had I not met Jane."

"Perhaps there's hope for you yet."

His gaze scanned the room. "At the moment, I am in the unhappy circumstance of searching out the most palatable wealthy partner with whom to spend my life."

She groaned. "Now you know what it's like to be a woman."

"Perhaps there's hope for you as well. I plan to aid in finding matches—"

Her laugh interrupted and carried to all the couples nearby. "No, no, Algie, please no. The last thing any of us wants is a profitable marriage." Her eyes sparkled with confidence and challenge.

He shook his head. "Only you would dare address me so. Here. But you wouldn't complain if the man you happen to fall in love with is also wealthy?"

"No, I wouldn't complain. But you may not see us around very much."

"You would just abandon your estate? Your family line? The tenants?"

A shadow crossed her eyes. "We might. I will admit the temptation is great. And you can't think I'm totally abandoning them all. I came tonight, didn't I?"

He shook his head. "When will I even begin to understand all of this?"

"I guess I can't expect much sympathy from you. You were there in the glorious future and came back to save the estate. Left the woman you love—I hear you loved her—and here you are. So my thoughts probably sound weak to you."

"I can very well understand. I wish you were staying. Having someone to talk to about . . . things . . . would be refreshing."

"You'll see me now and again. And we'll all be here for the wedding." Her eyes twinkled.

"Whose wedding? Mine? Perhaps you could point out the lucky lady so I can get moving on that?"

She just winked and then curtsied low and long. "Your Grace, it has been a pleasure seeing you again."

He took her hand in his. Then she grabbed it and held the finger with his ring. "You got your ring!"

"You vixen. Yes, I did. You are looking at a two-hundred-year-old artifact."

Her smile grew. "The best prank we ever did, that one." Then she turned from him and left Almack's as quickly as she could without drawing attention to herself.

Algernon was left with a new intoxicating feeling of hope. Something important happened today. He couldn't guess what exactly was the purpose in posing for the picture or why it mattered at all to Jane when they would never again be together, but he did know one thing, and that was that his own visit to the future had changed him, had motivated him to do all manner of things differently, and for that, he would always be grateful.

# CHAPTER 23

*J*ane worked hard on her thesis, on her doctorate paperwork, on preparing for her interviews, but she couldn't get Algernon's financial situation out of her mind. She checked back in with the articles now and again to see if history would again change itself. Such a crazy thought to have, that history could change. But everything had remained the same. He was well known and appreciated throughout the ages but had died almost penniless, the estate barely hanging on. Years later, those who came after would slowly begin to benefit.

She spent weeks completing her work, at the same time always on the lookout for information regarding the Lichfield or the Shelton estate. She couldn't get over the idea that both were connected somehow. The painting of her Regency Man hung in her home above the couch. His large smile welcomed her home every day from work, and she found herself back in the same situation she was in before she met Algernon, and that was living her life with the ideal man hanging in the periphery, a man who might as well be a fantasy because he lived two hundred years before.

Only now her ridiculous obsession was of course fed by memories of a real relationship with the man and a knowledge of just how incredible he actually was, not just fantasies about who he might be.

Day after day passed, as though in a dream, all her wishes coming true, mostly seeming unreal, but wonderful all the same. As each of her goals was reached, her doctorate paperwork completed, she felt their surprising lack in importance with no one to share them with, with no Algernon. Even her parents' excitement had dimmed in importance.

She sat at a dinner event where she had been invited as a guest speaker. She had excited everyone about the era, tried to bring it alive for them, showed pictures of the men from her auction and introduced a few of the ideas from her thesis, that women were doing the best they could, given what they had, but were a fair cross section of women you might find in modern times. They balked at the system like we do today and took a stand, fought for greater rights in the ways that were available to them. She touted Jane Austen as a revolutionary of her time, showed how her works proved these very same theories. People thanked her afterward. She was looking forward to the defense and then the publication of her dissertation.

Chelsea was thrilled that her historical society was getting more notoriety. The center certainly had plenty of funds for the next several years, and the others were fired up about improving the creativity of their own research.

Everything was going along better than Jane could have hoped, but she sat in frequent dissatisfaction. And the weight of doing something to help Algernon pressed down on her in her most quiet moments.

She had stumbled across an interesting shot-in-the-dark possibility one morning, and the dangling nature of the idea clung to her like a persistent barnacle. Rumors of smuggling activity along the Kent coast. She would have skipped right by it, except for the mention of the Lichfield sisters. She dug deeper into the smuggling activities along that coastline and found plenty of unsubstantiated claims of great troves of treasure, never recovered, hidden so well that once the smugglers died, no one came to claim it. And apparently the Lichfield properties were a hotbed location for a century of coastal activity. Smugglers, pirates, privateers, depending on who was paying them. They all used caves off the Kent coast as a base of operations.

Her mind began to swim with possibilities. And before she could stop herself, she was deep in a research rabbit hole about the smuggling habits off the Kent coast in England in the 1800s. She laughed at herself, but dug deeper. She knew this could solve everyone's problems. The women could be free to live without worry about finances on their own estate. Algernon could save his estate and actually see the fruits of his efforts in his own lifetime.

But the longer she looked, the more hopeless it seemed. People had searched for the treasure, and no one had found a thing. Perhaps the rumors were the reasons behind the brief Ramsbury attempt at a marriage alliance with the Lichfields. She could only guess.

She rested her head in her hands. If only they could find out what happened to that smuggler loot, if it existed at all. Then she whipped her head up, another idea coursing through her. Why not search ahead through the years? She had the benefit of hindsight. If anyone found any treasure during any decade, she could discover it now. And that stretched to any treasure anywhere. Her heart raced with possibility. A little ping reminded her she couldn't be stealing treasure. It would be best if some were actually located on the Lichfield land.

Hours in, again, when she should have been doing something for work, she sat at her cubicle, mapping out patterns of smugglers through the decades, marking known cave sightings and possible locations. Something about it was fun, like a real treasure hunt. And then she scrolled through a tiny newspaper article from Kent, over one hundred years old, detailing the looting of a smuggler's cave. No one could find any relatives of the family who owned the estate, all of them having disappeared or lost touch with society years ago, but the treasure was worth a considerable amount, the equivalent of many millions during the time it was discovered. And since the owners never came forward to claim it or put protection around it or guard it in any way, the looting continued until the cave was empty.

Her heart picked up. She clicked on the location, widening the map to see where it sat in comparison to landmarks nearby. Bingo! It was on the Lichfield property, along the shoreline not designated not by a known cave according to her maps. She jumped to her feet. "This is incredible!" Then she sat down. What could she do? She needed Nellie. No, she needed Anna. She could send Anna back to tell the sisters where the cave was. She called Anna.

She picked up on the first ring. "I knew you'd come back. Algie, where are you?"

"Uh, sorry, Anna. It's Jane."

"Oh. What is it, Jane?" She was never quite rude, but was never thrilled to hear from her either.

"I have some news that could save the Lichfield estate."

"They all said you matter," she said with as much disbelief

as Jane thought possible. "Have you at last found something?" She was quiet for many moments. "I'll meet you at Twicken-ham. The next full moon is in three weeks."

Jane took a deep breath. "Okay." She cleared her throat. "I'll call when I get there."

# CHAPTER 24

*A*lgernon's mother threw another dinner party at his home. Every eligible woman he had danced with at the last five balls had been invited. The requisite number of gentlemen as well, but everyone knew his purpose. Somehow, his thoughts were transparent to all. The awful financial state of things was becoming well known as he tried to clean up messes, pay off debts, and sell properties. A great tightening of all their expenses and a care for their tenants was likely noticed and added to the general understanding of his purposes. He felt good and productive in the industry and effort, but a general feeling of hopelessness that it would ever benefit his generation prevailed.

One woman at the table had a sufficient dowry to enable him to keep the main estate, his land, and his title. And she sat at his left, laughing overly loudly at his last comment, which was, "Lovely tarts. I wish all the functions we attend would serve tarts."

She was a handsome enough woman and seemed sensible, if not a bit too anxious to align herself with a duke's family. He felt twinges of guilt now and again that her lifestyle would not be the one she was probably envisioning, nor even like the one she now lived. Instead, their family life would be a much simpler affair while they waited for the estate income to rebuild. If he managed things carefully, the Ramsbury name would at least carry forward for many future generations. In order to accomplish such a thing, she would be gifting him an inordinate amount of money by way of her dowry for the opportunity to live in poverty so that he could save his estate for future generations.

He had asked to speak with her privately after the guests left tonight, and everyone knew what he would say and how she would respond. He grinned at her in response to her generous laugh and hoped they could carry on well enough together.

Then an express arrived.

He excused himself, paid the runner to wait, and tore it open. *All is saved. Don't do anything rash just yet. Oh, and Jane says hello.*

His hands shook. It was not signed, but he knew where to go. The full moon . . . He thought for a moment. He had taken to marking its growing and then waning phases. It was two days' past. About the time when the express would have been sent. Dash all the inconveniences of travel in his day! He called to a footman. "Ready my things. I leave at once for Chatwick Manor."

"Your Grace?" Lady Victoria Princley stood in the doorway, coming out of the dining room, her lovely pout wrinkled in confusion.

"Oh, my dear Lady Victoria. I must postpone our conversation. Perhaps indefinitely."

She gasped.

"No, it's nothing as morbid as all that. But I must make a last-minute journey, and I'm unsure how long I will be gone."

She nodded, and her lip quivered.

He bowed over her hand and kissed her gloved knuckles and then took off at a run up the stairs. Jane had sent her greetings. Did that mean she was here? At Chatwick Manor? Or did it mean the sisters had just come from there? Oh, confound it all. What did it mean? And why did they not have cell phones in his day? So many things had been a bother since returning home—about 1817 England—but travel and communication had driven him to distraction, as well as the inability to sit and have a sensible conversation with a woman. He supposed that had bothered him before he left, but it seemed even more troublesome now. There were precious few opportunities to speak with a lady in private, and within those, she stubbornly insisted upon discussing only certain topics.

His valet, Oliver, was efficiently and quickly placing clothing in his trunk.

"Hurry, Oliver. We haven't a moment to spare."

"Very good, Your Grace. I am almost finished."

At last they had everything and the carriage was loaded. His mother was attempting to calm her fits and frenzies, and he was off.

The journey might kill him slowly by painful monotony, but even though he felt like a snail could move faster, he *was* moving. He had sent a notice off, an express in return, notifying them he would arrive as soon as he could. And that he hoped to find *all* of them healthy and well. Could Jane have come? He asked himself the same question over and over again.

And then he counted the number of bumps in the carriage,

and then the number of turns they took, and then his breaths as he fell asleep.

At great length, when he thought he might burn away in a great fiery ball of impatience, they arrived at the steps of Chatwick Manor.

He took the front steps two at a time, didn't wait for the door to open, and announced himself. The place was quiet. No one responded to his abrupt entry. "Lady Anna!"

Silence responded. And he felt a draft. The housekeeper padded toward him. "Oh, is that you, Your Grace?" Her elderly voice made him smile. So many years she had helped him hide from trouble about this place.

"Yes, Mrs. Hollings, it is I. Are any of the ladies home? Lady Anna?"

"No, I'm sorry Your Grace. I haven't seen them for quite some time." Had she emphasized the word *time* or did he imagine it?

He bowed to her. "Thank you. I believe I shall pay a visit at Twickenham, then."

"Very good, Your Grace." She waited until he closed the door behind him to leave.

Then he rushed back into his carriage and had them urge the horses to the front of Twickenham. As soon as the door opened, a great laughter and the clinking of glasses caught his ear. "To another full moon well executed." Nellie's voice.

He followed the sound and entered the library. "Hello, Nellie!"

The room froze in its motions. His interest piqued at what he saw, the staff and Nellie in some form of toast, glasses in the air. Nellie lowered her glass and indicated he should follow her.

They left the library, and as soon as the door closed, he asked, "Is Jane here?"

She turned to him. "I'll bring you to the others. They can tell you the news."

"News? Is she all right?" His alarm grew. What could have happened? He realized how very much his own happiness depended upon the fact that she was well. How much he had so urgently desired to talk to her. How devastated he would feel if she were, in fact, not here.

The drawing room doors opened, and his gaze scanned the Lichfield ladies in the room. And stopped on Lady Anna, modern Lady Anna, dressed in a Regency gown, then the other Lady Anna, from his day. His smile grew, but his eyes scanned the room twice and did not see Jane. His shoulders slumped, and the ladies sighed, a collective noise that he found annoying. He thought his world would cave in on itself, his hope dashed so suddenly. "What?"

"You do love her." Lady Anna from the past looked to Lady Anna from the future. "You said it, but I didn't believe you until now."

"Excuse me, yes, of course I love her, but you don't need to discuss it in so callous a manner. Will you not greet me and explain what is going on?"

"Oh yes." The room as a whole stood and curtsied, and then a few murmured, "Your Grace." And then they sat, most trying hard not to burst out laughing.

"I'm not going to try to understand what has gotten into the lot of you, but I received a missive, an urgent one, desiring my presence, Jane was mentioned . . ." He widened his eyes. Hopefully this very tight-lipped bunch would at last disclose something of use to him.

"Oh, do sit, Your Grace." Lady Anna from his time indicated

a chair, and she stood. "I shall put you out of your misery. Your Jane did come. But she is no longer here."

His head fell forward into his hands, hope dashed. "What?"

Another sister, Constance, explained, "Yes, she insisted upon leaving again within the same full moon, though Nellie warned it can hurt twice as bad on reentry."

The future Lady Anna waved her hand. "She'll be fine, she has Advil."

The others nodded. And Algernon thought this the most eccentric meeting he would ever have. There were five sisters and one family member from the future all in one room. All beautiful, all strong. "And?" He waited.

"She came to deliver some rather spectacular news."

A few of the ladies grumbled.

"You don't seem to be too pleased with the news."

"Its delivery was given to us based on some contingencies which some are displeased with."

He huffed and waved his hand. With any luck, she would just continue talking and get it all out in one go.

"So, she gave us information on the location of a great amount of treasure on our property. So much treasure it would save our estate." The frowns increased, and Algernon didn't want to understand why they would be displeased with this news.

"But she would only release the exact location of the treasure if we promised to share it with you."

He was stunned. "She did this?"

"Yes, apparently your little Jane Sullivan feels something for you too. She's finishing off her dissertation this week and spent time traveling here with the news." Modern Lady Anna flicked her hand around as if her words were of no consequence.

"And back."

Algernon narrowed his eyes. "And if you're here, Lady Anna, why did she also need to come, if she's already gone?" His irritability increased more the longer he remained in the room with them. Jane had left. She must not care one ounce for him if she went to such great lengths to be gone before he could ever hope to see her.

"That was part of the agreement, I come and be witness to the contract we all signed."

Then he remembered the rest of the news. "What kind of money are you expecting to find?"

"Enough to save your estate for all the generations yet to come. She's saved you, Ramsbury. You can marry who you like, do what you like, the Duke of Shelton will last for countless generations to the front."

He sat back in his chair, allowing some of the realization of her gift to sink in. "So she researched out the location of a treasure, came here to tell you of it, and made you promise to share it?" He burst out laughing. "And is this why you are all grumbling?"

The Lady Anna from his time smiled. "Not all of us. You see, most of us don't live in this time hardly at all any more. We much prefer modern conveniences and the people we know in a future time. Our excuse for abandoning our family seat was that we had so little here we had little hope of it continuing on for much longer anyway. And we slipped away more and more until most of us are hardly here at all."

"Ah, and now?"

"Well, now we have received the means to save our properties, help our tenants, and do the dutiful and responsible thing."

Lady Anna from the future piped in. "Which I appreciate, since by our calculations, this could benefit me immensely."

They rolled their eyes, a gesture he had missed since returning home, and he almost laughed aloud. "So what are we waiting for? Let's go get us some treasure!"

They moaned. "We thought you would say such a thing. So we have called for extra footmen, the carriages, and for the house in Kent to be prepared. But we are still discussing amongst ourselves who will stay and who will go."

"Not all of you wish to stay, I gather."

"Absolutely not."

"Hmm." He nodded. "Well, if it would help you all, I have committed to work to find good matches for each one of you . . ." He let his voice trail off when he saw their expressions.

Lady Anna from his time smiled, "I don't believe that's the kind of support they need."

"True. Your Jane was very kind in her gesture, pointing out that since the estate is not entailed and we are now independently wealthy, we may do as we please. And choose to give the estate to anyone upon the last of us passing."

He was about to protest the lack of posterity and ask how would the modern Lady Anna come to be when the middle sister, quiet until now, held up her hand. "But some of us do desire a family, children, and a happy home here in this time, so this frees us up to make those choices." She sniffed and wiped her nose and eyes.

Lady Anna from his day whispered. "She's in love with someone in 1870 America."

He just nodded, the conversation more bizarre the longer he participated. He cleared his throat. "Well, whatever it is you do need. We have been friends a long time. I am learning that the salvation of my estate will be coming from treasure on your lands. I will do what is in my power to assist you."

"Thank you." Lady Anna from his time stood. He joined her, and she came to stand beside him. "We will all go to Kent, see what is in the caves, and determine how to divide it up equitably. The estate will take all of the remaining share after Algie has his." She turned to her sisters. "Once you receive your share, then we are all free to make up our minds the course we will take from there."

They nodded.

The Lady Anna from the future met his gaze. "I decided to stay. I wanted to see your face." She winked. "Catch it on my cell phone."

The ladies all sighed.

She turned to them, "What, you don't bring your cell phones?"

They shook their heads.

He felt a bit self-conscious and then asked, "How is everyone? Lord Smithing and the lot of them? Charles? The Band of Brothers?"

She shook her head. "I'm sure I haven't the slightest idea how your biker gang is faring, but the others are well; Charles has taken to yachting with us and Trent."

"Ah yes, the large Trent."

"He's been visiting England of late." Her face colored prettily, and Algernon was happy for her.

He didn't ask about Jane, but they all knew he wanted to, so after a moment he gritted his teeth and spit out, "And Jane?"

"She's doing well. Seems happy now that she's done this for us, for you." Lady Anna didn't say more, and Algernon wished to shake the information out of her. But how could she know? Jane wasn't likely to tell her how much she loathed him.

Though she certainly didn't loathe him if she'd gone to such great lengths to save him. But why hadn't she stayed?

"I think she feels her place is there. Or she will until she completes her dissertation and things. Then after that?" Anna shrugged.

And a spark of hope lit. Perhaps she would return.

# CHAPTER 25

*J*ane stood in front of the auditorium hall full of people. She had been awarded her PhD, and they had asked her to be the concluding speaker at graduation that year for the university. She ended her speech with something her fascinating time studying Regency England had taught her. "No matter where you live, no matter who your people are, there is great power in the individual. You bring to your life unique circumstances, things that would never be there if you weren't. So be that something. Be the you inside that no one else can offer, and make the past, present, and the future richer because you were in it. Thank you."

She smiled out into a standing-ovation crowd. And she felt complete, mostly. Chelsea stood and cheered, and the whole office of their historical society joined her. Jane felt great satisfaction that she had saved their society, had published new and innovative research, and had brought to light further understanding of women, a further appreciation of them.

They went out to dinner. And she celebrated with everyone. At one point they toasted her and she dipped her head in acceptance of all their cheers. She felt incomplete. No, that wasn't totally accurate. She felt complete, done. The great peace of a job well done, but it was over. Nothing sat on the horizon. Nothing waited, and she just couldn't think of a single thing her life held for her particularly. The irony of her speech was that she could think of no way her individual talents were further needed.

She went home and continued on with work for several weeks before she got a text from Anna. *I'm back.* And then she sent Jane a stream of text pictures of Algernon, of his face when they told him the news, of the cave full of smuggling valuables, of the group of sisters, and a selfie of her and Algernon entirely too cozy. But she had to laugh. He held his hands out in a sideways peace sign. She hugged the phone to her chest. Aching for the sight of him. She had done it, saved his estate and Lady Anna's. And at last, hopefully, made up for her awful treatment of the man she loved. Yes, loved. She ached for him like she would her arm, her own lungs, her heart. *Thank you.*

She expected nothing further from Lady Anna. The woman was nothing if not sparse in communication. But her phone dinged again. *Well? Are you coming?*

*Coming where?*

*To visit? Your dissertation is finished.*

She thought, counted to ten, and then texted back. *Yes! See you in two days.*

A celebration. She deserved it. And when she clicked on the airline webpage to reserve her flight, she asked for 1A.

ALGERNON WENT HOME A WEALTHY MAN. He loaded two

carriages full of items from the cave, two trunks of gold coins, silks, French wine. The cave seemed to hold booty from the time during the French wars and before. He wondered what had happened to the owners of the items. Or perhaps the Lichfield family was involved in the smuggling, perhaps the knowledge died with the death of their father. Whatever the case, he rode on his horse, surrounded by his paid armed guard and several footmen, back to his estate. The relief that filled his heart burned through him, taking all the worries of the past six months away with it. And what remained felt clean, hopeful, and at peace. And almost complete.

One thing lacked. A gaping absence in his heart where Jane used to take up residence. None of the sisters could fill what she had given him. He had spent time over the last couple weeks getting to know them again, joking, playing, working, conversing. While each of them was strong and independent and spoke her mind, he found nothing in them that completed his needs like Jane had. When at first he thought he could have been enamored with just the idea of her, he now knew that he loved not the suggestion of Jane, but Jane. The very essence of her. And no one would ever be the same or complete him like she had.

But that was such a lonely thought. And he tried to push it aside as he rode back in celebration of a vibrant and wealthy estate. He would stop sales on all properties he had planned to lose, pay off all remaining debts, and begin investing in ways to earn more money. If not for his missing Jane, he would be the most pleased man in all the world. Free to marry for love at last, but the love of his life wouldn't be born for another two hundred years.

What an absolutely insane thought that she had entered his time for the space of an hour and then left. For one hour she had been standing in the year 1817. And he hadn't even known.

When he arrived home, he called the staff together, announcing raises for them all and thanking them for their incredible patience through many years of questionable financial troubles. They cheered for him, he broke open a bottle for them all, and then he went off to his chambers.

He dismissed his valet. Of a truth, he enjoyed the privacy of a life without servants. He wouldn't live that way forever, but at times like these, he craved the solitude. Then he sat at his table and brooded. He had no other word for it. His eyebrows furrowed until he got a headache, and he mulled over all the many ways his life would be better with Jane in it.

But he couldn't return. He had a responsibility here. He knew what had happened when he neglected his estate, and he simply could not do that again. *But Jane.* She loved his time period. She spent her life studying it. Had even come here once. She was done with her dissertation, her life's work completed at her young age. He laughed. He didn't even know how old she was. Was there any chance at all that she'd come to live here? What did he offer in 1817 that she wouldn't laugh at from her position in 2019? But what kind of man would he be if he didn't try, if he didn't at least ask?

An energy filled him. How many weeks until the full moon? Two more. Perfect. Thoughts turned into the semblance of a plan. He would continue to get his new wealth organized and then make arrangements to be at Twickenham on the full moon once again. He would go to her, convince her to come back. His heart clenched. What woman would want to do such a thing? He could only try.

## CHAPTER 26

As soon as the airplane doors opened, Jane was the first to get off the plane. She raised her hands in the air and walked down the nearly empty exit ramp. *Victory.* She made her way to baggage claim and felt a smile stretch across her face when a driver held up a sign with her name on it. "Lady Jane."

She collected her bags, and the driver took her to Chatwick Manor. Driving across the same countryside she had traveled when she journeyed back to Regency England just a few weeks ago brought all the familiar anticipation. But she told herself she was not hopping two hundred years this trip. She was going to relax in the year 2019. So there was nothing to feel anxious about.

Actually standing in the Regency time period had been surreal. She had hurried so that there would not be the temptation to stay, gave herself just enough time to deliver her message, sign agreements, grab a memento, and go. She smiled as she fingered a slip of ribbon—*1817 ribbon.*

And she had celebrated when she made it back without

weakening in her resolve, without seeing Algernon. Oh, it hadn't been easy. She had hungered for him, her hands shaking with hope that somehow he would have guessed her intent and would be standing at Twickenham Manor waiting to hold her in his arms. But no. He had an estate to save, caves to ravage, and a wife to find. She couldn't stand in where she did not belong any more in his life. She grinned to herself, thinking of the pictures Anna took of his discovery of the caves.

When she pulled up in front of Chatwick Manor, she wasn't surprised to see Lady Anna. They had only recently become close; the woman had a hard time getting over the fact that Jane was born a commoner. But since her last visit, when Jane literally saved her estate, Anna had taken to texting and conversing with her as old friends.

As soon as the driver opened Jane's door, Anna squealed. "I just found out I own a foundation."

Jane laughed. One of the interesting parts of Anna traveling during the smuggling find and visiting the caves was that when she returned home, she could see the changes that had happened all around her situation. "I saw Algie has increased his holdings as well."

"Yes," she waved her hand, unconcerned as ever with the plight of others. "I help with literacy now too, and I'm thrilled about it. It's amazing, Jane, what you did for our family."

Jane smiled. She at last felt at peace about the way she left things with Algernon. His estate was famous around the world for the good it did, stating its reasons stemmed from two hundred years ago when the Duke of Shelton set out the expectations for their family and its wealth. By his own ducal decree, they were to share ten percent of their fortune always, forever. "I'm even happier about helping you all than I am about saving our historical society and my own dissertation." She laughed and then air-kissed Anna on the cheeks.

They hurried inside, arm in arm, and Anna told her all about the plans for that evening. Jane was not quite the partier that Anna was, but Charles would be there, and she was excited to hear what he would do with all of the research she had forwarded on to him. After her big splash so strongly proving the strength of this family of daughters, he couldn't very well come out and try to prove the opposite. But she couldn't be sure. So she wanted to discuss their research, which she knew Anna would find incredibly boring.

Jane laughed at something Anna said. "How is Trent?" What an unusual turn of events. Never would she have guessed that Trent and Anna would even hold the slightest interest in each other, ever, but here they were, bouncing back and forth across the ocean to spend time together.

"He's lovely and fits right in with everyone. You won't care if he comes, will you?"

Jane shook her head. "No, I'm way beyond Trent."

"True." She sighed. "I imagine, once you've won Ramsbury's heart . . ." She wiggled her eyebrows.

"Now that's just cruel." But she couldn't help smiling, even if it was awful to act as though they had even the tiniest modicum of a chance together.

"Oh, come now, the full moon is in just a few more days."

"And?"

"Well, and . . ." She stopped and grabbed both of Jane's hands and stared into her eyes, her expression daring, sparkling, full of challenge. "You should go back. And this time, spend some time, at least a month."

Her heart skipped and pounded, and she had to place a hand at her chest to remind herself to breathe. "But what good would that do?" Her face started grinning before she could even stop herself. "I can't stay forever . . ."

"Can't you?"

*No.* How could she just up and leave her time? Her century? But to see Algernon again, a whole month in Regency England? She didn't know if she could resist such a thing.

Anna squealed. And Jane had never seen her behave so . . . normally. "You are totally doing this! Oh! I want to come! But I can't this go round, that last travel made my head ache for weeks."

Jane didn't care what it did to her head. Now was the perfect time for a vacation. And especially one where no one would notice she had gone. But did she dare? The more she thought about it, the more she knew she just might.

## CHAPTER 27

$\mathcal{A}$lgernon approached the entrance to Twickenham Manor. To think, three months ago, he had never cared to enter the smaller manor, and here he was arriving for the third time in so many months at their front door.

It swung open for a young man running down the drive, shouting back over his shoulder, "I'll return at the full moon."

Algernon shook his head. Would he ever be surprised about what he found at Twickenham? He suspected not.

He peeked into the hallway. This time, the house was bursting with people, all in costume. It appeared to be a masquerade ball. Well, this certainly complicated things. All he wanted was a word with Nellie and a possible visit to see Jane. If he dared. Which he might. But he had to be absolutely sure he could return. So much was at stake now for his estate. Perhaps if he traveled to Jane, he could convince her . . . dare he even hope . . . dare he even put to words his thoughts? Convince her to come back with him. Yes. He had to try. He wanted Jane in his life.

He pushed through the crowd, everyone in masks. He

grabbed the nearest person, "Have you seen Nellie?" The masked guest shrugged.

People would point in a general direction, and he would follow. A woman stepped closer. "Oh, Your Grace. I'm so happy to see you again." Her voice sounded familiar, older, but he couldn't place it. She giggled and nudged the lady at her side. "I won him, fair and square, one evening. Fifty thousand dollars."

He gasped. The woman at the auction? But she moved past, greeting people all around her. At last he thought he saw the back of Nellie's white hair. He moved in that direction. But a woman stood in his way, in costume. "It's me. Lady Anna."

From his time. "Oh, Lady Anna, I just want to see Nellie. I've got to go back to Jane."

"Come with me." She led him in the opposite direction he'd seen Nellie go. Many called to Lady Anna as they passed, and she waved cheerfully back in response.

"Who are all these people?"

"Those who are about to travel or who have been. Nellie invites a group of us every full moon." She moved the mask away from her face. "I don't think she's expecting you."

"No, she wouldn't be. Does it matter? I would very much like to go back to see if I can convince Jane to . . ." He swallowed. "Live here."

"Let's get you on your way."

"Can you do that?"

"Well, no, but I can at least get you in the right place."

They walked up the stairs, and it gradually quieted. Algernon appreciated leaving the loud chatter behind because he needed to think, to concentrate.

They took another set of stairs farther up into the house.

Lady Anna said, "So we'll go back into the painting room. You'll have to show me which one is yours."

He opened his mouth to express his confusion when Nellie joined them. "Hello, Your Grace. Thank you Lady Anna. I'll take it from here."

She smiled. "Good luck, Algie. You deserve to be happy."

He smiled a nervous half smile. Now that Nellie was here, he felt more anxious than he had expected. Going to another time accidentally was one thing, but purposefully traveling again seemed quite a different degree of brave altogether.

"You, of course, haven't been up here yet. This is where most people come and go through time."

"Do they do it differently than I have been?"

"Most do, yes. They enter through their paintings, usually."

"So, I could do that now, enter through a painting and go back?"

She nodded. "You could."

"And if I convince Jane, could you bring us both back to this time again?"

"I can. More or less."

"More or less? Is that a yes or a no?"

She ignored him and opened up the door to what looked like an enormous art gallery. He followed her in, mouth open at all the different portraits. He could only guess they had all traveled through time. Some day he wanted to sit this woman down and get some answers. But he suspected you only got the answers she cared to give, when she wanted to give them. She led him to a mirror, so tall it reached to the ceiling, and she left to get his painting.

She brought over a large canvas and uncovered it. But in doing so, a huge flash of light filled the room and grew in intensity right around the mirror. He thought it would be hot, but it was cool. He hesitated to look right in its center, but found that he could, without any trouble. He was filled with a yearning to enter this light. Everything else in the room was invisible to him, as if the light consumed it all. He stepped closer, staring. A figure started small, at the back of the light, and moved toward him. The light flashed with a greater intensity, not brighter, not hotter, just more, and the figure moved closer. Jane!

He rushed to her, met her in the center of the light. It lifted the ends of his hair, filled his body with energy, but all he focused on was Jane. He pulled her into his arms. She felt soft against him. And she smelled amazing. He buried his face in her hair. "Jane, my Jane." The light flared all around them, blocking out anything but the two of them.

"Algernon. I came to you."

"Wait, you did? I thought I came to you."

They looked around. Jane wrinkled her lovely nose, and he had the strongest desire to kiss it. And then her lips. "Then where, or I guess when, are we?"

He pulled her close. "When would you like us to be, Jane? I can't live without you."

She looked up into his eyes, put a hand at the side of his face, and said, "Wherever you are. I'm here for a month, maybe forever."

"Make that forever, Jane. If you will, if you can leave all in your time, I will make you a duchess, give you as many ball gowns as your heart desires, and teach you every tiny Regency detail you've been wondering about."

Her eyes widened, and he hurried to continue before the fear crept in.

"But even more, I will love you, Jane. I will treasure you and hold you as something precious to me, for as long as we both live. I want you at my side. Jane, will you marry me?"

She choked, the light around them continued, and then she searched his face. "Yes. Oh yes! Algie, I will marry you."

The light doused. And they stood in Nellie's upstairs room.

"That took you long enough. I've been standing here trying to decide to what time I was sending you both." Nellie stood with hands on her hips, both paintings at her feet.

"Nellie!" Jane smiled. "I just left you in 2019, and here you are. I won't try to understand how."

She held up her hands. "Just enjoy each other. Come back if you ever want to go back to your birth time, Jane, grab a hotdog on Fifth and Broadway." She winked and then left the room.

Their eyes followed her out of the room. Then Algernon turned his attention back to the precious woman in his arms. "Did you just agree to marry me?"

Her face broke into a huge smile. "I did."

He ran a thumb along her lower lip. "I couldn't be happier, Jane. If you're sure . . ."

She stood up on tiptoes and reached up to grab the back of his neck. His heart thrilled when he felt the pressure of her soft lips on his. He mumbled against her mouth, "Mmm. Welcome to Regency England, Lady Jane Sullivan." Then he responded to her searching with an insistence of his own, angling his mouth to capture the most of hers he could, over and over, pulling her up against him, thrilling with the thought that the Jane he thought he'd lost was back and had agreed to be his. "Mm. Wait. I have a confession to make."

She tipped her head. "What?" Her lovely eyebrow rose in a delicious arc he wanted to kiss back down into place.

"I got a tattoo."

Her mouth opened wide, wider than he'd ever seen it go. "You what!"

"I did. I can't show you now, it's in one of those places, but I will, that is, when I can, when we are . . ."

"Married?" She laughed. "I cannot believe it. Was this when you were out with Anna?" A slight dissatisfaction crossed her eyes. Which he hurried to erase.

"No! Of course not. No, the Band of Brothers and I got matching tattoos: 'Band of Brothers.'"

She held a hand to her head. "I really cannot believe it. I'm tempted to take a picture of it for posterity's sake just to freak out all the historians of my day."

"Henry V, you know."

"Yes, I know." She shook her head, stepped back, and took a good look around the room. Then she squealed, running to the window. "I'm here. Last time I could not appreciate it properly."

"Oh, last time. Jane." He followed her and reached for her hand. "I thank you. You have saved my estate." Then he grinned. "Well, I suppose it's fitting, for it will now be our estate. Jane, you've saved your own estate, and the estate for our children." He pulled her close again, and her eyes widened with such a look of love and hope he couldn't help but press his lips to hers all over again. "I love you, Jane."

"And I love you too, Algernon."

# EPILOGUE

$\mathcal{H}$e carried Jane in his arms into their London townhome. They'd planned a wedding celebration to take place in three hours, but first, there was the matter of the letter. He set her down and then pulled out the aged and faded envelope.

Her eyes widened. She took it carefully in her hands and ran a finger over her name. *Jane.*

"Should we open it?"

"Of course." She slid her finger carefully along the edge and broke the seal, then unfolded the paper. She laughed in amazement, shock, sucked in a huge breath of air and choked on it. Handing it to Algernon, her eyes filled with tears. She couldn't speak for her amazement and joy.

He read it aloud. "Dear Mom, well done. We love you and Dad. Signed, Your Children." She leaned over his arm to stare at the words together, tears from both their faces falling on the paper.

"Oh, careful, we must save it."

He lifted the paper with one hand and then cradled Jane's face in his other. "Our children."

"I know." Her heart felt like it might burst with happiness. Then she paused. "But I don't know how comfortable I am letting our children time travel. I mean, is that really such a wise move?"

He laughed and led her into his home. "We can worry about that later. First, I want to show you something." They went to the front parlor. A huge painting filled one wall above the settee.

"My Regency man." She grinned. The very painting that had introduced her to Algernon.

Then he pointed out the side windows. "See that tree over there?"

She turned to him and shook her head. "Is that?"

"A sugar maple. I have a good feeling about this."

"I'm sure you do."

Sign up on her website for her newsletter to get freebies, contests, prizes, and first news. http://www.jengeiglejohnson.com.

Or to Join her ARC team, follow her FB group.

Other historical books by Jen:

The Nobleman's Daughter
Two lovers in disguise

Scarlet
The Pimpernel retold

Tabitha's Folly
Childhood friends. Four Protective Brothers

Damen's Secret
The villain's romance

Dating the Duke
Time Travel: Regency man in NYC

Anthologies
A Christmas Courting
A Yuletide Regency
To Kiss A Billionaire


CHECK out these fun Sweet Contemporary Romance Titles:
The Swoony Sports Romances
Hitching the Pitcher
Falling for Centerfield
Charming the Shortstop
Snatching the Catcher
Flirting with First
Kissing on Third


HER BILLIONAIRE ROYALS SERIES:
The Heir
The Crown

The Duke
The Duke's Brother
The Prince
The American
The Spy
The Princess


HER BILLIONAIRE COWBOYS SERIES:
Her Billionaire Cowboy
Her Billionaire Protector
Her Billionaire in Hiding
Her Billionaire Christmas Secret
Her Billionaire to Remember


HER LOVE and Marriage Brides Series
The Bride's Secret
The Bride's Cowboy
The Bride's Billionaire


HER SINGLE HOLIDAY Romances
Taming Scrooge

Made in the USA
Las Vegas, NV
02 March 2025

18936469R00136